GOOGLE EYES

by
Willard Helmuth

Royal Fireworks Press

Unionville, New York
Toronto, Ontario

To Karen

Royal Fireworks Press
First Avenue
Unionville, NY 10988
(914) 726-3333
FAX: (914) 726-3824

Royal Fireworks Press
78 Biddeford Avenue
Downsview, Ontario
M3H 1K4 Canada
FAX: (416) 633-3010

ISBN: 0-88092-070-X Paperback
       0-88092-071-8 Library Binding

Cover Illustration by Mary Patricia Arnold.

Printed in the United States of America by the Royal
Fireworks Press of Unionville, New York.

CHAPTER ONE

Barney Google

"Grandma! Mums! Joe's here! We can eat now," Dee shouted as she ran into the kitchen of the cottage.

"Dorothy! Keep your voice down!"

The stern command from her grandmother only made Dee grin. She knew it was not the loudness that bothered her, but Dee's insistence on calling her father by his first name. Dee and the nervous old woman had never gotten along too well together. They both knew it was not supposed to be like that. Grandparents were supposed to spoil their grandchildren rotten, take their side in family arguments and tolerate their every whim. Grandchildren were supposed to adore it.

Grandma Oster, however, was always trying to discipline Dee, and Dee seemed to always be able to irritate her, often without even trying. Like the business of the names. Dee always called her father, Joe. Her mother was Mums. Her calico cat, for reasons no one seemed to know, was named Donkey. Grandma thought nicknames were silly. She always called Dee by her given name, Dorothy.

It wasn't so much that Dee didn't like her name as much as that it just seemed so old-fashioned. It always brought up an image of Kansas and the Tin Man, even though her parents claimed they had given no thought to the Land of Oz when she was born. She had actually been named after her great-aunt. That made it even worse.

So over the years it had become shortened to Dee. That was easy enough for her friends and even her teachers, although, of course, she always had to explain it on the first day of school each fall. The only people who called her Dorothy were the substitute teachers and Grandma.

Actually, Dee really thought of her name as just plain D. That way she could match her monogram to whatever mood she had that particular day. Most of the time she was Decent and somewhat Deliberate; some days she was even Delightful. But there were times she could be Destructive and even Disgusting.

Once, she had heard her grandmother call her a "problem child." At the time she didn't know what that meant, but much later when she did understand the meaning she refused to accept the label, possibly because the words didn't begin with a D.

Other people tried to stick labels on her, too. The worst person was Billy Snodgrass. He called her Google Eyes, which she supposed was a variation on "goggle eyes" for the thick glasses she wore. He said it just to get her mad. Sometimes he and his jerky friends would taunt her with a stupid song.

Barney Google,

With the goo-goo-googly eyes.

Barney Google,

Had a wife three times his size.

She sued Barney for divorce.

Now he's living with his horse.

Barney Google,

With the goo-goo-googly eyes.

The song was just silly and a lot of the other kids sang it, too, but the verse Billy made up was cruel.

Dee-Dee Gardner,

With the goo-goo-googly eyes.

2

> Dee-Dee Gardner,
> Yes, she has four eyes.
> Watch her stumble when she walks.
> It's a wonder she can talk.
> Dee-Dee Gardner,
> With the goo-goo-googly eyes.

When Billy would sing it, she felt like hitting him and running away at the same time. She never had the nerve to actually hit him, and if she ran away she probably would stumble, so she usually just stood there and called him Billy SNOTgrass. When the other kids called him that he flew into a rage and started throwing chalk and erasers. When Dee called him Billy Snotgrass he just laughed.

Mums told her once that if she would just ignore Billy he would probably stop teasing her. But she couldn't help it. Every time he did it she started shouting before she could even remember Mum's advice.

When she was in the first grade, she overheard her teacher discussing her "handicap" with her mother. Ever since then she hated the word. It was like she wore a T-shirt with a skull and crossbones, or had red stickers plastered on her forehead that said: DANGER! RADIOACTIVE MATERIAL. For a long time she lived in fear that they would have to get special license plates for the Toyota, the ones that had little wheelchairs in the corner.

What she really wanted was to be Normal, but that didn't begin with a D either, so she supposed it wasn't possible. Then on days when she really felt Down-in-the-Dumps, she sometimes wished she was really handicapped, a real cripple so she could shock people with her monstrous Deformity. Instead she was always just Dee; Dee with the thick glasses and the stumbling walk.

3

From the time she realized she was different from other children, Dee wanted to know why. She pestered her mother to tell her what had happened to her, but for years she would only say, "You were a premature baby, Dee."

Then she would get a sad look in her eyes and say no more.

It was not that Mums was a bad parent. Dee knew that she loved her very much. It was just that sometimes it was hard to talk to her about some things. So Dee stopped asking her about her eyes, just like she stopped asking why Grandma Oster always had to come along on these family vacations. She found it much easier to talk to Joe.

One evening she and Joe went for a long walk along the shore. They sat on a rock watching the sandpipers darting back and forth, playing tag with the waves and snapping up little sea animals from the sand before the fickle ocean could rescue them. She felt especially close to her father that night. They had spent the day building sand castles and fishing from the long pier that ambled out into the water on scarecrow stick-legs.

They sat in silence on the rock, hand in hand, until the sun set behind their backs. They listened to the sounds of the sea below them and felt the tingle of the spray against their bare feet.

"Joe, what happened to my eyes?" she asked suddenly.

"It was something that happened to you when you were born, honey," he replied.

"I know that," she said, "but what happened?"

"It was because you were a premature baby," he told her.

"I know that, too," she persisted. "You told me that much before. Exactly what did that have to do with it?"

4

Joe seemed surprised at the question. He hesitated as if he thought a twelve year old wouldn't understand his answer.

"The oxygen you were given hurt your eyes," he explained.

Just then Mums and Grandma came walking along the shore and the conversation came to an end. The answer stirred both an uneasiness and an excitement in Dee. She knew what oxygen was. She had learned about the element in Miss Charnick's sixth grade science class. But she didn't understand what that could have to do with her eyes. She wanted to ask Joe more about it later that week, but somehow the right opportunity just never came up.

The word oxygen stayed in her mind, flashing on and off at odd moments like the neon signs along the boardwalk. She promised herself she would learn more about oxygen when she got home.

CHAPTER TWO

The Library Search

Monday morning she was up early. Joe had left for work and Mums was still asleep. Mums always slept late the day after vacation. Dee hurriedly dressed and slipped the stems of her thick-lensed glasses under the tight beginnings of her braids. Then she went down to the kitchen and wolfed down a bowl of slightly stale Cocoa Crispies before jumping on her bike and pedaling down Crestwood Drive.

At the stop sign she swung right onto Central Street, past the park and past the Pathmark store with its summer supply of watermelons and lawn fertilizer strangely intertwined on the sidewalk.

As she approached the bike rack of the library, she scarcely noticed it was empty. It wasn't until she raced to the door, her empty Snoopy bag flowing from her shoulder, that she realized the library was closed.

She dug into her jeans pocket, came up with a quarter and a nickel as well as some sand from the ocean, and crossed the street to the Dunkin Donuts shop. The counter was lined with twelve upright newspapers. Twenty-four pant legs dangled beneath. Every so often a hand would sneak around a paper to clutch a coffee cup or a Krispy Kreme.

Dee found a stool in the far corner and patiently waited her turn. Finally a grumpy waitress with hairpins in her stringy bleached mop loudly asked for her order. Dee winced, for she never could get used to people raising their voices whenever they saw her thick glasses. She bravely ordered a beehive, then stuck out her tongue at the wide backside and saggy stockings when the waitress turned away. It was an act of impulse and she quickly glanced around, certain she would be turned in for waitress abuse. None of the newspapers stirred.

She still fumed as she slowly chewed the beehive. She had seen old people treated the same way. People always thought that since they were elderly they were hard of hearing. But it made even less sense to her why people should talk loudly just because of her glasses. It made her want to shout at them, "It's my eyes, you ninnies. My ears are okay."

Once, she and her mother were in Aldens to buy shoes. The only shoes Dee liked weren't available in her size and the clerk became irritated and started speaking louder and louder. Suddenly, Dee took off her glasses, placed them against her right ear like an old-fashioned hearing aid and said, "Eh? What's that you say, Sonny? I can't quite hear you."

The astonished clerk only stared at her and her horrified mother whisked her out of the store and straight home. That was one of the nights Dee heard whispers of "problem child" between Mums and Joe.

It was even worse when people treated her as if she were Dumb. Fortunately, that didn't happen so often anymore. When she was younger, she had worn leg braces. When people saw her slow walk and thick glasses, they concluded she was mentally slow. Well, she was no retard, that she knew for sure, but it was terribly painful when she was treated that way.

Mums had told her that her leg problem had also come from her premature birth. "Born too early," was what Mums called it. She explained that most babies were born nine months after they first began to be formed. Dee was born after only seven months. Then Mums had changed the subject again before Dee could ask more.

Now her stiff and unwilling legs had gotten much better. The braces were forgotten in the attic, along with the crutches she had used for awhile after one of the operations on her ankles. She knew her walk was still not normal. It was most noticeable when she tried to run with the other girls around the track at school, and sometimes she would stumble for no apparent reason. Still, she could ride her bike, walk to school and even play tennis, although she wasn't very good at it.

The clock on the wall said 8:01, so she licked the last sugary crumb from her fingers, tucked her crumpled napkin under her plate and left the donut shop.

She was the first person in the library. She felt right at home, for every few days she rode her bike here to fill her Snoopy book bag with novels by her favorite authors.

Today, however, she rushed up to the second floor where the reference books were stacked. She followed the alphabet of the card catalog, looking for the O's. "Ow - Pain" was on the top row. The card catalog was so tall that she had trouble reaching the handle and she almost spilled the cards as the drawer tumbled out. Getting it back would be another problem. She leafed through the index cards. Oxford. Oxley. Oxhorn. Oyster. No oxygen. She checked again just to be sure.

"Stupid library," she muttered. "They don't even have it."

At once she realized her mistake. This was only a branch library. She would have to go to the main library downtown to find a book about oxygen. Then to her horror she saw a librarian standing beside her.

She's heard me, Dee thought. Now she will think I'm Dumb. She quickly looked for a way to escape, but the card catalog blocked her way to the stairs and before she could sneak off and get lost in the book stacks the cavernous mouth would open and the tirade would begin.

Oh boy, Dee thought, here it comes. She will shout at me and tell me the braille books are downstairs.

Instead all she heard was a soft voice that politely inquired, "Could I help you find something?"

Dee's eyes followed the gray slacks and print blouse past the name tag that said "Miss Vaughan" and ran smack into a sweet smile.

"You're new here," Dee blurted.

"Yes," the smile replied, "it's my first day. Now, how can I help you?"

"Ox-oxygen," Dee mumbled, embarrassed by her rudeness. "I-I need a book about oxygen."

"Hmm," Miss Vaughan said, "let me have a look." She glanced through the drawer Dee still clutched in her sweaty hands. "I guess we don't have any books about just oxygen."

Dee suspected the lady knew that before she even looked.

"Have you checked the encyclopedia?" Miss Vaughan asked her.

Again Dee felt Dumb. The encyclopedia! Of course! The lady must think she was a real ninny.

But the librarian was still talking to her. "It might be a place to start, but I'm sure you'll want to read more than you will find there. I tell you what. We have a whole series of children's science books. They probably have something about oxygen. I'll get some of them while you check the encyclopedia. Do you know where it is?"

Dee nodded. She didn't feel quite so Dumb now.

Oxygen came right after Oxyechus vociferus and before oxynotidae. Dee took just a minute to skim the short sections about the killdeer and the prickly dogfish, then read the passage about oxygen sandwiched between.

Many of the words were too hard for her to understand. Something about ions and elements and atomic numbers. She glanced at the rest of the page and a picture caught her eye. It showed a premature baby receiving oxygen in an incubator. She wondered if she had once looked like that.

Miss Vaughan returned with a stack of books. "Here you are," she said, handing them to Dee. "These should have something about oxygen in them. If you need any help I'll be at my desk."

Dee spent all morning looking through the books, first finding "oxygen" in the index, then flipping the pages back and reading the text.

When it was time to go home for lunch she checked out as many of the books as she could stuff into her Snoopy bag. She spent the afternoon under her favorite oak tree in the back yard reading and sipping lemonade. Even Donkey was ignored as he tried to curl up on her lap. He finally gave up and went off to stalk butterflies in the rose garden.

CHAPTER THREE

A Magic Cure

The next morning she was back in the library. Miss Vaughan said hello to her as she walked through the door and made a remark about her beautiful hair. The compliment pleased Dee. Her hair was beautiful. She had long blond braids that wavered in the sunlight. Yesterday, Miss Vaughan seemed not to notice Dee's thick glasses. Dee had thought perhaps she was one of those people who seem to look right through you, seeing nothing. But today there was no chance that was so. Miss Vaughan had seen her face, had noticed her long braided hair, but seemed to find nothing unusual about her thick glasses.

By the end of the week they were friends. Together they located books about oxygen. Dee read all of the books, spending the mornings in the library and the afternoons under the oak tree.

She couldn't believe how much there was to learn about just one small element in the universe. Oxygen seemed to be everywhere. It is in the air we breathe, but then everyone knows that already, she thought. She learned that it made up over three-fourths of the ocean, most of it combined with hydrogen to form water. It seemed to be present in one form or another in just about everything around us. She followed its pathway into the lungs, through the blood stream and into the body cells where something called metabolism took place, changing the oxygen into other chemicals and releasing heat. She was surprised to learn that this "oxidation" in the body was similar to what happened when a log or a piece of paper was burned.

She read that the Chinese recognized the existence of oxygen nearly a thousand years ago but that it was not isolated and named until the eighteenth century. She was intrigued by the experiments of a man by the name of Lavoisier, although she really didn't understand them all that well.

Everything she read about oxygen indicated it was good. That puzzled her. It was necessary for life to almost all plants and animals. When people got sick with pneumonia or heart disease, doctors gave it to them to help them get better. She couldn't understand how something that good could have hurt her eyes. None of the books she read even mentioned anything about oxygen and the eyes.

Then one day something happened that made her forget about oxygen for awhile. It was hot and humid when she left the library and by the time she reached the park she was tired and thirsty. She bought a Sno-Cone at the Mister Frosty truck parked on the street and stretched out under one of the giant maple trees to eat it. She pulled a Trixie Belden book out of her Snoopy bag and was soon deeply engrossed in the adventure.

Suddenly she became aware of the conversation of two elderly women on the park bench nearby.

"Oh yes, Cora, it's wonderful how I can see now."

"And you were only in the hospital for a few days, Maude. It's amazing what they can do these days."

Dee crept closer, not wanting to miss a single word.

"Yes, it sure is. Imagine! Transplanting things from one person to another. Who would ever have believed it possible."

Dee listened with growing excitement to the description of the operation. She wanted to run up to the women and ask where she could get a transplant, too, but their crackling, stern voices made her afraid they might be angry that she had eavesdropped on the conversation.

Instead she jumped on her bike and pedaled home as fast as she could, Trixie Belden and the Sno-Cone completely forgotten. Mums would know where to get a transplant.

But Mums wasn't at home, so she spent the afternoon under the oak tree, drinking lemonade and telling the good news to Donkey. Donkey purred in reply, but seemed unimpressed.

An eye transplant! Of course! Why hadn't she thought of it before? She had heard about a man in Utah or somewhere who had gotten a heart transplant. Or was it an artificial heart? She couldn't remember which. And there was a little girl in her home town who had gone to Pittsburgh or somewhere for a liver transplant.

The idea had always seemed gruesome to her, taking parts out of dead people and sewing them into living people, but now suddenly it didn't seem so icky. She wondered how you went about getting the eyes. Did you have to go out and find a dead person yourself or did the doctors do that for you? The thought of sneaking around in a graveyard in the middle of the night picking out a pair of eyes made her giggle. Then she looked at Donkey's green slit-like eyes and wondered if they ever put cat eyes into people. That seemed even funnier to her.

She planned to announce the wonderful news to her mother and father at dinner that evening, but as they sat down to eat, Mums said, "Don't forget about your appointment with Dr. Scribner tomorrow morning, Dee. I'll drop you off on my way to the dentist."

Dr. Scribner was Dee's ophthalmologist. Dee couldn't pronounce that so she just called her her eye doctor. She had forgotten all about the appointment, but now a new idea flashed into her mind. She would talk to Dr. Scribner tomorrow about having an eye transplant, then surprise Mums and Joe with the good news tomorrow night.

All that evening the excitement in her grew. She remembered how scared she was when she had the operation on her ankles, how frightened she was of the anesthesia mask just before she went to sleep. This time it will be different, she thought. This time it would be so good to have her eyes fixed that she wouldn't even think about being scared of the surgery.

She even planned a party for all of her best friends. They would pop balloons and eat strawberry swirl ice cream and chocolate fudge cake. Then they would take turns jumping up and down on her old thick glasses, crunching them into thousands of pieces of glass and plastic.

The excitement was still there when she awoke the next morning. She hummed along with the music on the radio as she slipped on her Levis and Esprit shirt.

The waiting room was full of impatient people when she got to Dr. Scribner's office. At first she was dismayed but when the receptionist told her she was late because of emergency surgery, she accepted the delay.

As she waited her turn she had a fantasy of the receptionist addressing the people in the waiting room saying, "I'm sorry to keep you waiting, ladies and gentlemen, but today Dr. Scribner is performing an eye transplant on her favorite patient, Dee Gardner."

At last it was Dee's turn to be seen. A visit to the eye doctor was interesting and even kind of fun. She never did anything to hurt her and the array of equipment to test the eyes was fascinating. But today Dee was impatient for the exam to be over so she could ask Dr. Scribner her important question. Because of her impatience she hardly noticed that

Dr. Scribner looked tired and hurried and didn't tell Dee any of her usual jokes and riddles.

"Okay, Dee, your eyes are the same. I'll see you again in six months."

She turned to go and was almost out the door of the examining room before Dee could blurt out, "Dr. Scribner, I want to have an eye transplant."

Dr. Scribner paused and looked at her curiously. "Did you say an eye transplant?"

"Y-yes," Dee stammered. "I don't mind going through the surgery. It would be worth it not to have to wear these stupid thick glasses and to be able to see better. Please, Dr. Scribner, I'm sure my parents would let me do it."

Dr. Scribner walked over to her and gently put her arm around her shoulders. "Dee, that is not the problem. You see, we can't transplant the whole eye. We can only transplant the front parts of the eyes. The retina, the very back part, of your eye is damaged. We can't transplant that part of the eye."

She had tried to say the words as gently as possible. Dee really didn't understand what she was saying about the different parts of the eye, but she certainly did understand when she said she couldn't have an eye transplant. The meaning came to her with the harshness of a cold winter storm. The tears welled up inside her but she fought them back until she reached the safety of the oak tree. There they rained down on the soggy coat of a bewildered Donkey.

CHAPTER FOUR

Down in the Dumps Again

For two weeks Dee was Discouraged and Dejected. She spent most of her time locked in her room or under the oak tree sobbing her disappointment to Donkey. Donkey purred in reply, offering sympathy to his sad friend.

Mums and Joe tried to coax the reason for her bad mood from her, but she remained silent in front of them, trying not to let her feelings show. In an effort to cheer her, Joe would pop her into the Toyota and drive her to the Dairy Delight for double dip strawberry swirls with sprinkles, but that only made her happy for a few minutes.

One day a card came from the library. It was a reminder that her stack of unread books was past due. Dutifully, she stuffed them into the Snoopy bag, scrounged a few coins from her porcelain sea gull bank with the words "Souvenir of Ocean City" on it, and pedaled toward Central Street.

She had hoped to drop off the books, pay her fine and depart quickly, but to her dismay, Miss Vaughan was at the front desk that day. Dee almost bolted for the door, intending to drop the books in the night return slot, but Miss Vaughan had already seen her and Dee was afraid she would think she was trying to avoid paying the fine.

Miss Vaughan smiled and said, "We have missed you, Dee."

"Uh, I've been busy, Miss Vaughan. How much is the fine?"

"Let's see. It is fifty cents. But I tell you what. Since this is the first time you've been late returning your books, I won't charge you."

"Thanks," Dee mumbled. But she plopped two quarters on the counter anyway and turned to make her escape.

"Dee, come here a moment."

Oh boy, thought Dee, I'm Dead. Why did I have to be so rude? Now I'm really going to get yelled at. She felt like she was in first grade again, about to be punished by her teacher like the time she put a gushy night crawler down Billy Snodgrass' back.

She returned to the desk, unwillingly.

"Dee, it's your eyes, isn't it?"

Resentment filled up inside her at once. So Miss Vaughan had noticed all along, Dee thought. She brought it up to punish me for being so rude.

But the tone of Miss Vaughan's voice told her she had been wrong once again. "That's why you wanted to learn about oxygen, isn't it, Dee?"

Dee just nodded her head and dabbed a tear from the corner of her eye. Stupid eyes, she thought. They can't even hold tears in place.

"Dee, how would you like to have lunch with me? I'll call your mother and ask her if it is all right. I can leave in about fifteen minutes. You can look through a few books until I am ready."

Dee wasn't certain she wanted to go, but she didn't know how to turn down the invitation without being rude again. Besides, Miss Vaughan didn't give her a chance to answer one way or the other. Before Dee could think of an excuse, she had given Miss Vaughan her phone number and the arrangements were made.

A short time later they were on their way to the park. They bought two hot dogs from the funny street vendor who played a harmonica for his customers, then sat under the same maple tree of eye transplant history. Miss Vaughan emptied the contents of her brown bag to share the lot. She produced an orange and two halves of a peanut butter and mayonnaise sandwich. Dee could only stare in amazement, for she had never met anyone else in the whole world who liked PB and M sandwiches. She thought it a taste affliction somehow associated with defective eyes and unwilling ankles. But Miss Vaughan had no crutches and didn't even wear glasses.

Contacts, Dee thought. I bet she wears contact lenses.

"Do you wear contacts, Miss Vaughan?" she blurted. Oh boy, she thought, there I go being rude and nosy again.

But Miss Vaughan didn't seem to think the question was unusual. "No. I am very lucky. I only wear glasses for reading sometimes."

Somehow Dee didn't think that was enough to account for her PB and M taste, so she forged ahead with another meddlesome question.

"What about your ankles? I mean, uh, they are very pretty ankles, uh, I mean, uh, did you ever break them or anything?"

It was a stupid question and Dee knew it. She was being Dumb and Disgusting again, but somehow she just couldn't help it.

"No, Dee. I did fall out of a tree when I was six and had a skull fracture."

That's it, thought Dee. The bump on the head messed up her taste centers.

Miss Vaughan changed the subject. "Tell me, Dee, what else would you like to know about oxygen? Would you like to learn how it hurt your eyes?"

The question was so direct yet so sincere that all of Dee's defenses crumbled. All of a sudden she didn't care if she acted Dumb. Here was her big chance. Here was someone willing to help. She wanted to jump up and shout YES. She wanted to hug Miss Vaughan and promise to repay her with a thousand and thirteen PB and M sandwiches. But all she could do was nod her head. She hoped Miss Vaughan would not interpret the gesture as a lack of interest.

"Good," Miss Vaughan said. "We will start tomorrow morning. But don't expect the answers to come quickly. This may take a lot of time and research."

That evening Dee was almost as excited as the night she had learned about eye transplants. The disappointment of that venture was nearly forgotten. Somehow she was certain that in knowledge she would also find a cure.

The search was disappointing at first, but then Miss Vaughan had said it might be. They looked through dozens of library books, selecting every possibility from the card catalog, then carefully picking the pages from the index of each book. They went through Vision, Eyes, and Blindness. They concentrated on the name doctors had given to Dee's eye disease, retrolental fibroplasia.

Dee had heard Dr. Scribner use the words, but they never had much meaning to her before. Now she repeated them over and over again in her mind, syllable by syllable, ret-ro-len-tal fi-bro-pla-sia. The words danced about in her head like a catchy TV commercial that stuck with you all the more when you tried to push it aside.

They found little aside from the name and a few crisp sentences about prematurity and oxygen, things that Dee knew already. She again began to feel the panic of failure.

But Miss Vaughan was not in the least bit discouraged. "It's what I expected, Dee. You know, I can find you a book about fixing a car, or an explanation of how a nuclear power plant works. There are hundreds of books about computers and others about space, but for some reason there are few really good books written about our bodies. It is going to take a little more work, but I know where we can find the answers."

CHAPTER FIVE

Back to the Library

The next day when Dee arrived at the library, Miss Vaughan had her wait in the reading room until her lunch hour. Then they got into her car and drove to the hospital across town. Dee recognized the place at once and it brought back unpleasant memories of the taste of anesthesia gas and the unrelenting pain in her ankles. This time, however, they marched right past the dreaded admissions office and entered a door marked MEDICAL LIBRARY. Dee was introduced to Mr. Weston who obviously had been expecting them.

"I didn't get any articles for you yet," he told Miss Vaughan. "I thought Dee might be interested in seeing how we find them."

He walked over to a computer and explained, "This terminal is connected to another computer at the medical school in the state capital. They keep a record of all recent medical articles. I'll request a listing of all the articles about retrolental fibroplasia in the English language published in the past five years."

Within minutes the little dot-matrix characters spilled out onto the paper that slowly unraveled from the printer. Dee was astounded to see so many references about her eye disease, especially since there had been so few at the public library. She asked Mr. Weston about it.

"Oh yes, scientists are very interested in the problem and are still doing a lot of research. But remember, these articles are all written for doctors and nurses. We will have to find some that are written so you and Miss Vaughan can understand them."

He glanced over the list in front of him. "Here are some that look like they may be helpful. I'll get the journals and make photocopies for you. I'll also make copies of the chapters in some of our nursing and medical textbooks for you."

He hesitated, then looked from Miss Vaughan to Dee. "Are you sure this is how you want to learn about your eye problem? Sometimes people get mixed up when they read medical articles. Maybe I could get one of our nurses to talk to you instead."

Dee shook her head vigorously. "No. Please. I want to try to find out this way first. Maybe later I could do that."

Miss Vaughan agreed. "The best way to learn is to dig out the information yourself. And I'm willing to help her understand the difficult parts."

A short time later they left the hospital armed with a stack of still-warm photocopied pages. Together they spent the next few days plowing through each article. Some were just too difficult for either of them to understand, but others were helpful.

With Miss Vaughan's help, Dee gradually learned some things about what had happened to her eyes. She learned that the eyes of premature babies, like most of their organs, are not fully developed at birth. Because of this, oxygen, usually harmless to other people, can damage the retina, the back part of the eye, causing scars to form. Even with Miss Vaughan's help, Dee did not understand how the oxygen did that to the eyes. In her mind she envisioned the oxygen acting like a sharp knife cutting her retina and leaving jagged tears like the ones on her knee after she had fallen on a broken Pepsi bottle when she was nine.

"Then why did the doctors give me oxygen?" she mumbled, scarcely aware she had spoken the words aloud.

"Dee, it says here that most premature babies have trouble breathing and need that oxygen," Miss Vaughan told her. "I guess that means the oxygen can be both good and bad."

Dee was not satisfied with the answer. "Why couldn't they have used something other than oxygen to help me with my breathing?"

"I don't know, Dee," Miss Vaughan replied. "I think maybe Mr. Weston was right. We should talk to someone who knows more about this. Let me talk to your mother. Maybe she can arrange for Dr. Scribner to talk to you."

Dee had told Miss Vaughan about Dr. Scribner, but she had never mentioned the episode of the eye transplant. She couldn't face Dr. Scribner again, and she really wasn't comfortable talking to Mums about it, either. She did not feel like explaining all this to Miss Vaughan, so she just shook her head and said, "No, I want to read some more before I do that."

Reluctantly, Miss Vaughan agreed. "Okay, Dee, but remember I'm going to be away on vacation for three weeks. When I get back we will talk about this again."

Of course, Dee had not forgotten about Miss Vaughan's vacation. She was going to England, and when they were not talking about oxygen and Dee's eyes, they spent the time talking about London, the Thames, the changing of the guard at Buckingham Palace, and the quaint cottages in Somerset. Miss Vaughan had promised to take lots of pictures and tell Dee all about these places when she returned.

The next day Miss Vaughan stopped by Dee's home to tell her good-bye. Before she left she handed her a book.

"I thought you might enjoy reading this. I bought it several years ago but now I want you to have it."

The book was titled Climbing Blind. It was written by a French woman who had been blind since she was two years old. The book described her adventures of climbing in the Alps; scaling rocky cliffs, crossing dangerous crevasses. Dee was amazed that a blind person could even learn to scale mountains, but the most interesting parts of the book were the author's descriptions of the mountains, based entirely on her touch, her hearing and the vision of her companions.

Dee lay under the oak tree gazing at the sky above her. She had finished the last page and still clutched the book against her chest. Her thoughts swirled in her head like little sandstorms on an ocean beach. She knew she was luckier than the author of the book. Yet, she thought, it is no fun wearing thick glasses and even with them my eyesight is not very good. Still, she felt guilty about feeling sorry for herself when others were totally blind.

She gazed at the clouds drifting above the fluttering oak leaves, trying to sort out her confused thoughts. As she watched the sky, she heard the drone of a distant jet, then watched its progress across the sky. Its twin vapor ribbons drifted into long fleecy cirrus clouds that finally scattered into a misty haze.

Suddenly, she sat up. The book slid to the ground and was forgotten as it sprawled across a dusty, gnarled root. Airplanes! Mountains! The association flashed in her mind. She raced to the house and yelled to Mums that she was going to the library.

CHAPTER SIX

The Big Plan

This time she ignored the card catalog and headed right for the Nepal-Pasteur volume on the far right side of the encyclopedia shelf under the window. Nuclear energy. Ocean. Ohio. Oriental art. Owl. Oxygen. She didn't even look at the picture of the baby in the incubator or read the paragraph describing the chemical composition of the element. She skipped right to the last few sentences on the page.

> Mountain climbers take along a tank of oxygen which they must breathe, because there is less oxygen in the air high above the ground. High-flying airplanes also carry a supply of oxygen to use when it is needed at unusually high altitude.

She returned home and again took out the stacks of medical articles Mr. Weston had copied for her and re-read the now familiar words. There could be no doubt about what she had read, but to be certain she went over it again and again until the words blurred together in the watery reflection of her aching eyes.

Her conclusion had to be right. Since oxygen was hurting her eyes, she would have to live somewhere where there was less oxygen. Of course, she could go around with a paper bag over her head all day and spend the night locked in a stuffy closet. But why do that when there were the mountains? There the air was crisp and clear, deficient in oxygen yet containing enough for life.

She had a vision of living high on a majestic peak, watching clouds drift below her, feeling the distant valleys slowly come into focus as her eyes gradually healed. She knew it was not a crazy idea. After all, Heidi had taken Clara to the mountains to be cured, and she thought she remembered stories of other people who took trips to the mountains for their health.

The idea was so simple that she wondered why it had never occurred to her before. Somehow she never questioned why the medical articles didn't mention this cure.

Once again Dee had a plan. She considered sharing her discovery with Mums and Joe, but some stubborn streak made her keep it to herself. Maybe somewhere deep inside a warning was trying to sound, telling her that it was another foolish idea, but she never let that little voice reach the conscious level of her mind.

Now her days in the library were spent with the M's, reading about all the great mountain ranges of the world; the Alps, the Himalayas, the Rockies, the Andes. Every picture of a mountain hut nestled among the wild flowers excited her more and more.

But all of these mountains seemed so far away. How did one get there? She couldn't just pack a knapsack, kiss Mums and Joe good-bye and set off on her bike for the Pyrenees.

Maybe the whole family could move to the mountains, but then that meant Joe would lose his job. Maybe he could find new work there. He could be a lumberjack or a forest ranger while she and Mums made wild blackberry jam and blueberry muffins to sell to the tourists. It would be a big change from Joe's job as a computer programmer, but she was sure he would do it for her.

Of course, that meant she would have to tell him about her secret. She wasn't quite ready to do that yet. Besides, although she wouldn't admit it, there was still that small nagging possibility that she might be wrong. She dared not think about that. She was certain the mountain air would cure her eyes. She just needed to prove it to herself and her parents.

So she came up with the perfect solution; a vacation in the mountains. If she could just spend a week or two there, her eyes would improve a little bit. She was sure of it. She would then share the wonderful news with Joe and Mums and they could plan to move there for the rest of the cure.

Joe had another week of vacation coming soon. He planned to stay at home and do some work around the house and in his garden. Since they had already spent a week at the ocean, there was no money to travel again. But Dee reasoned that a camping trip would be inexpensive. Mums hated camping, but Joe loved to camp and fish. Dee began to plan her strategy.

A road map of the eastern United States lay sprawled out on her bedroom floor. It was an old map, used more often for dreams of journeys than to navigate along winding roads. The folds were ragged and in places rivers and highways had been bridged with little pieces of yellowed Scotch tape.

She found the Blue Ridge Mountains in Virginia. Joe had hiked the Appalachian Trail there years ago and still told stories of catching trout in the sparkling mountain streams. She looked for the map scale in the lower corner and spread her thumb and index finger to approximate fifty miles. It was nearly eight finger spaces to Virginia. Too far.

There were the Green Mountains of Vermont and the White Mountains of New Hampshire. Again she finger-walked her way across the map. They were too far away, also.

She found the Catskills. They were close by, but somehow they didn't seem like real mountains to her. None of her friends who had been there had ever talked about climbing any high peaks.

Then there were the Adirondacks, a great big area carved between Canada and the New York Thruway. The map was peppered with blue patches between mountain peaks. There seemed to be an unending number of little triangles marking the location of the highest summits with names like Haystack, Puffer, Kunjamuk and Ampersand. Beside each triangle was a number that she knew represented the elevation of the peak.

Now a new problem occurred to her. How high would she have to go before her eyes would be cured? Most of the Adirondack mountains had an elevation of about four thousand feet. She knew that meant they were that far above the level of the ocean. She remembered that Joe had told her once that the oak tree was about fifty feet high. She tried to imagine eighty oak trees stacked on top of each other. She decided that four thousand feet was plenty high enough. The Adirondacks it would be. Now to convince Joe to take her there.

Some children would have run up to their father, given a big hug and the kind of sloppy kid-kiss that parents never seem to mind, and beg to go on a camping trip. Dee was more clever than that. She spent the next two days in the library reading all she could find about the Adirondacks. She read books, magazines and newspaper articles. Then she was ready. At dinner one night she had her opportunity.

As usual, the topic of discussion was the nuclear power plant that might be built near them. Joe was once again voicing his opposition and reciting the potential danger the plant presented.

"I agree," Dee chimed in, "but there are dangers from coal burning plants, too. Look at all the acid rain they are causing and the damage it is doing to the lakes in the Adirondacks."

Her statement had definitely gotten Joe's attention. If there was anything that upset him it was pollution, especially if it damaged fishing spots.

"It is interesting, though," Dee continued, "that while nearly all the fish have died in some of the lakes, other lakes seem to be unaffected. Conservationists say the bass fishing has never been better in some places."

"You know, I always did want to fish in those waters," Joe remarked. "I hope I can do it before the whole area is ruined."

"Why don't you go on your vacation next week?" Dee suggested. What she really meant was why don't we go, but she thought it wiser to get Joe hooked on the idea of fishing first.

"Oh, Dee, I'd love to, but we said no more vacations this year."

"But it wouldn't cost much," Dee persisted. "I figured out it would cost about thirty dollars for gas. There would be a small fee for camping in the state park, but the Johnsons said we could borrow their tent and camping equipment and the Wolinskis are willing to let us use their boat. Of course, we would have to buy groceries, but we have that expense at home, too. Besides, I'm willing to give up my allowance for a few months to help pay for the gas."

The words she had planned so carefully had just sort of spilled out on top of each other. Dee had presented her whole argument at once before realizing it. Oh boy, she thought, I messed up again. I was going to let Joe get used to the idea gradually. Now I've probably made him angry.

But Joe was laughing. "Hold on a minute, young lady. What is this *we* business? A minute ago this was a fishing trip for me. You little sneak. You were tricking me into this, weren't you?"

Dee knew Joe was only teasing her and was pleased with what she had arranged.

"Okay, Dee, I suppose it is possible," Joe continued. "But what does your mother have to say about all this?"

Mums, too, was laughing. "Oh, I think it's a great idea. But please, just the two of you go. You know how much I hate camping."

And so it was settled. The next week Dee and Joe would go camping in the Adirondacks.

That night Dee cuddled Donkey next to her on the pillow and whispered visions of mountain peaks and placid lakes.

CHAPTER SEVEN

The Camping Trip

Dee slammed the trunk lid of the Toyota, grinning at the whoosh of compressing blankets and over-stuffed grocery bags. A tell-tale strawberry and lime shoelace from her old sneaker protruded from the crack. She let it be.

"No more room there," she remarked, and surveyed the pile remaining on the sidewalk.

Somehow it all fit in the back seat except for her travel bag of goodies. She noticed with pride that there was even a jagged little valley in the center so Joe could still use the rear-view mirror. The outboard motor was on the floor of the trunk and the boat was already strapped to the luggage rack.

She ran back into the house and shouted, "I'm ready, Joe."

They were off before daybreak and were well out of town before the drowsy morning sun even peeked above the meadows. They had chosen their route carefully, finding the paved but lightly traveled roads and avoiding the boring interstate highways. Joe was pilot, Dee the navigator with folded map propped on the open glove compartment door.

She followed their journey marked on the map with a yellow felt-pen line, calling out each new route number and announcing every town. Part of the thrill of the trip was watching tiny map circles evolve into 35 m.p.h. speed limits, Sunoco stations and frame houses with picket fences.

They had breakfast at a small diner, having intentionally avoided the fast food chain restaurants with their precooked, microwaved food stuffed into Styrofoam boxes. Dee struggled through a hugh stack of thick-sliced French toast and juicy sausage patties. Joe had his usual two eggs over light, rye toast, tomato juice and coffee.

The waiter, who was also the cook, the gas station attendant, and the owner, leaned against their booth and told fishing tales of the Adirondacks. Then a customer at the counter chimed in with stories of salmon snagged from some river with an exotic sounding Indian name.

Dee could have listened to the conversation all day, but it was time to spoon up the last bit of maple syrup and be on their way. Joe gave her five dollars and she went to the cash register to pay for the meal, because that was fun. As the man gave her the change, he slipped her a Snickers bar and promised her a milk shake on the return trip.

They passed through little towns that resembled their foreign namesakes by their title only; Paris, Rome, Russia, Poland. At this last town they stopped at a country store for soda pop. Joe said it was almost the way stores were when he was a little boy, before the days of the giant self-serve markets. Rows of groceries were stacked on shelves that extended from the bare wooden floor. A candy jar filled with red and black licorice stood on the checkout counter. The cash register was the old-fashioned kind that gave a pleasant ding as the dollars and cents sign popped into the little window at the top.

The soft drink cooler was a type Dee had never seen before. She tried to find the slot to insert her quarters. Joe laughed and slid back the metal lid, telling her to pick out what she wanted. She peered at the assortment of grape, orange, and colas, all in returnable glass bottles. At Joe's suggestion she chose a Nehi cream soda. As they sat on the steps sipping the delicious tangy beverage, she felt like she had stepped into another country or an earlier time.

Now it was north and west again on winding roads that passed farm ponds with swimming Mallards and crossed little streams on one-lane bridges. Once they took a short cut; a faint blue line on the map with no name or number and an uncertain destination near, but not quite at, a town called East Bloomfield. The road became narrower and narrower. The potholes increased in number. Dee wondered if East Bloomfield even existed, for there was no Bloomfield on the map for it to be east of.

The road ended at a T. She wasn't certain if she was pleased, disappointed, or simply having too good a time to care one way or the other that they were lost. But an old man in a lawn chair in front of a mobile home directed them to "the four corners" and soon East Bloomfield became a reality. It was a vacant Mobil station and a cinder block Pentecostal church with a yard full of children emerging from the morning session of Bible school.

When they finally reached the Adirondacks, it was almost a disappointment. Only a wooden sign separated the weedy fields of the state park from those of private land, but then the terrain changed quickly and they passed rocky streams and pine-wooded hills. In the distance the peaks were barely visible through the haze.

At noon they reached their destination, Little Squaw Lake. The ranger welcomed them as if they were personal friends. She showed them a map of the grounds and offered them a choice of hundreds of different campsites. Some were beside the lake, some beside a trout stream and some deep in the woods. They all sounded neat to Dee, then she became even more intrigued as the ranger described which sites were most likely to be bothered by bears.

They drove all around the area, then selected an isolated spot in the woods but also right next to the lake. It was separated from the main campground by a narrow sandy lane.

Dee thought the spot was perfect, well, almost perfect. It was a long walk to the bathroom, but she didn't care too much about that. It was also rated as low risk for bears. She had mixed feelings about that. She was torn between a fear of being shredded in her sleeping bag in the middle of the night and the excitement of actually encountering one of the burly monsters.

She jumped out of the car and ran to the water's edge. She gazed at the islands in the lake, the nearly hidden campsites on the far shore and the mountain peaks rising from the near horizon. She selected the highest peak, majestic in its rocky expansion. When she removed her glasses it became an indistinct blob, merging with the cloudless sky.

She smiled, put her glasses back on and returned to the campsite. That mountain would be her focal point.

CHAPTER EIGHT

Lookout Mountain

They set up the tent together, first spreading out the ground cloth, then neatly stretching the floor with the aluminum stakes and finally assembling the poles at each end. It was incredible that a few pounds of fabric, stuffed into a small bag, could expand to an enclosure big enough for the two of them to stretch out in their sleeping bags with room enough for a third person in between. It made Dee feel like she was on a Mt. Everest expedition.

While Joe made lunch, she read the pamphlet the ranger had given them about the bears. There were sobering precautions that made her glad they had chosen the "low bear risk" campsite. All garbage had to be carried out to the bear-proof cans by the road after each meal. All food had to be locked in the car trunk. No crumbs were to be left around the campsite. The final warning convinced her of the cunning ability of the bears to sense food. The person cooking the evening meal was advised to change clothes before going to bed at night.

It was not the bears that invaded them first. As they sat by the picnic table eating their hot dogs and potato chips, a trio of chipmunks appeared from the underbrush. When Dee saw the first one she quietly tried to lure him with a piece of potato chip gently tossed in his direction. The caution was hardly necessary. He rapidly ate the chip, then he and his two friends scampered right to Dee's feet, begging for more.

"Oh, aren't they cute," she exclaimed. "And look, one of them doesn't have any stripes."

Sure enough, he was a strange variant, denied his trademark by an accident of his heredity.

"You start feeding them and they'll never leave us alone," Joe cautioned.

But when she begged, "Just a little bit more?" he didn't have the heart to refuse her.

After lunch they unloaded the boat from the top of the car and slid it into the water. Its path left a little ditch in the sand that looked like a garden row waiting to be planted with corn or string beans.

They left the outboard motor behind this time and Dee took the oars. She was clumsy at first and they zigzagged on a crooked course that seemed to get them nowhere. But she was determined and Joe was a patient teacher. Soon she had the rhythm and the bow sliced neatly through the gentle waves.

Joe fished for bass, casting his rapela minnows and brightly colored rooster tails into the shallows, grunting in pretended disgust whenever he snagged a sunken branch. Dee was content to fish for the little bluegills and perch, dangling juicy fat worms over the stern, letting her sinker hit bottom, then reeling in two turns.

Neither of them caught anything. It mattered little. The lake with its reflection of mountain peaks, the fresh air and the company of father and daughter were rewards enough.

"What time is it, Joe?" Dee asked.

"Three-ten," he replied.

Fifty minutes to go, she thought. By some undetermined reason in her mind, the first test of her vision was to occur at four p.m. Exactly four p.m. as if minutes or even seconds could make a difference.

She asked the time so often that Joe asked if she was getting bored, so she quit at three fifty-five and counted slowly under her breath to three hundred. She slipped her glasses casually from her face and gazed to the east. The mountain was more clear! She was sure of it! It still looked like a blob of lime Jello spilled on a blue tablecloth, but this time she could recognize it as a mountain. This time the image was more clear.

She put her glasses back on, thinking, it's working. This air with less oxygen is curing my eyes. It's working!

Then she wasn't so sure. Was the image really more clear or was that just her imagination? She took off the glasses to check again and couldn't decide. Glasses on, glasses off. Glasses on, glasses off.

"Are you all right, Dee?"

"Oh, uh, sure. Uh, my glasses are dirty," she mumbled, and quickly started to wipe them with a corner of her T-shirt.

Joe looked at her strangely, but said no more. After that she didn't dare take them off again.

Supper was Spam and macaroni and cheese cooked on the Coleman camp stove. For dessert Dee made banana cream pudding, doing her best to squash the lumps from the instant mix as she stirred it into the milk.

They walked hand in hand to the bear-proof garbage can, then watched the sun sneak behind the mountain. She thought of it now as her mountain, for she didn't even know its proper name.

They played gin rummy by the light of the lantern. Dee won, 1026 to 483. Then they crawled into their sleeping bags, glad for the warmth of the down-filled layers, for the night air had become chilly. Joe told made-up stories of goblins and hobbits until Dee's laughter became sleepy yawns.

That night Dee dreamed of being a forest ranger, watching for forest fires from a tower high on her mountain. She could see for miles and miles and didn't even need a telescope to pick out little clearings, small ponds and the distant hazy peaks. Then on the far horizon she glimpsed just a tiny wisp of smoke. Quickly, she telephoned the location and soon water-spraying planes and helicopters filled with fire fighters had come to the rescue. The blaze was extinguished before any real damage was done and Dee received a reward for her sharp observance and quick action.

She was awake at five-thirty and fumbled for her glasses in the near darkness. She slipped out of the tent and went down to the water's edge. Her favorite peak loomed from the far shore. It was blurry in the faint morning mist with her glasses on, unrecognizable with them off. She was not discouraged. She knew it was only because of the morning haze and the lingering night that she could not see it clearly.

She tried to make pancakes for breakfast. She and Joe both laughed when they turned into sticky lumps that clung to the pan. Even soaked with maple syrup, they looked and tasted like leftover mashed potatoes.

They spent most of the day fishing, winding their way among the many islands, dropping their lines in promising spots. This time the fish were biting. For awhile all Dee had to do was to drop her line over the side and they took the bait even before it hit bottom, announcing their capture with little Morse-code tugs on the line. Dee played a game of seeing how many fish she could catch with one worm, making each piece smaller and smaller and taking care not to dislodge them from the hook when she caught a fish.

Most of the fish were too small to keep and she gently freed them, wondering if they scurried off to the safety of a weed patch or greedily rushed back to nibble at her hook.

They kept the larger ones and placed them in a wire fish basket hung over the side of the boat. When the sun got warm and the fish stopped biting, they reclined in the boat and read their books.

Dee read a short funny novel about a boy who was constantly in trouble in school because he was always pretending to be a race car driver. She giggled at the description of him as he made the sounds of gears shifting on an S curve.

Dee was glad her eyes were good enough for her to read. Her doctor had explained that she had myopia, or nearsightedness. That meant she had the most trouble seeing things at a distance. Even when she wore her glasses the scenery was somewhat blurry when she rode along the highway. She also couldn't see anything out of the corners of her eyes. Dr. Scribner said that was because she had poor peripheral vision. She knew she could never be a race car driver. She probably could not even drive a car when she got older, she thought glumly, unless, of course, the mountain air cured her eyes.

Again she slipped her glasses off after making sure Joe wasn't watching her. But Joe was involved in a big thick history book about the Russian Revolution. The mountain looked the same. Or did it? For a second she thought it was more clear, then a moment later she decided it was less clear. The horrible thought occurred to her that for some strange, cruel reason the mountain air was making her eyes worse.

The thought frightened her and for the next hour she lay on the floor of the boat, all interest in reading and fishing lost. Then the fish started biting again and that cheered her a little. She hooked one that struggled and tugged and threatened to break her line. She slowly reeled it in, following Joe's instructions to let it play with her line until it tired. Joe had to use the net to get it in the boat. It was a lake trout, a full twenty inches long. Joe said he was proud of her and by his smile she knew he meant it. For the moment Dee forgot about her eyes.

They fried the fish over an open campfire that evening. It tasted better than anything she had eaten in her entire life.

Joe promised her a different kind of fishing for the next day. After supper they walked to the ranger station to get directions to a mountain stream. The ranger gave them a map of the whole area that showed the trails, the streams, the lakes and the mountains. Dee looked at it carefully that night and identified each landmark she could see from the campsite. Her mountain now had a name, Lookout Mountain.

It was such a common name for a mountain. Many people would have considered it ordinary and unromantic. But the name gave new meaning to Dee's search. It was a symbol of the change she was sure would come to her vision. It would be like the mountain in her dream. From there she would be able to see forever.

CHAPTER NINE

Another Grand Scheme

They were awakened in the middle of the night by a strange rumbling sound that sent chills up and down Dee's spine. She thought it must be the mating call of an East African bull elephant, although she had never heard the mating call of an elephant and the smell of balsam and fir told her she certainly wasn't in East Africa.

"Bullfrogs," Joe whispered.

At first Dee didn't believe him, but as she listened again to the unmistakable croak, she had to agree. Then they heard another sound. It was the loud bang of a door and the rattle of metal.

They both identified the source at once. "Bears," they announced to each other.

Dee snuggled close to Joe and whispered, "I'm scared."

"Oh, they are way up by the road," Joe reassured her. "They are only trying to get into the garbage bin."

Her fear was replaced by an impulsive bit of bravery and curiosity. "Let's go see them."

"No, no, Dee. The ranger told us to leave them alone."

But Dee was insistent and Joe, too, had to admit he was curious, so they quietly crept along the sandy lane using their flashlights as little as possible. When they reached the road, the moon came out from behind a cloud and they could clearly see the bear attacking the garbage bin. He looked huge to Dee. She was sure he was a giant grizzly. Joe told her he was only a medium sized black bear, but then what did a computer programmer who read history books know about bears.

41

Again and again the bear forced his paws against the door, but even this brute lacked the strength to push it open very far. When he let go, the spring clanged it back with a bang. Dee almost wished she could go help him, to show him how easy it was to open if you pulled the lever the right way. At last he ambled off in search of an easier meal.

In spite of their middle-of-the-night adventure, they awoke at dawn again. Dee barely had time to check on Lookout Mountain, with and without glasses, before it was time for breakfast. Once again she had trouble determining if it had become more clear or not, but was so eager to go to the trout stream she decided to wait until the afternoon to try again.

They followed the lake shore to its narrow southern end, then walked along a twisting rocky trail. Dee had a little trouble walking here, but Joe was patient and knew better than to suggest they turn back. As they made their way through the woods, they heard the stream gurgling in the distance. They went through swampy underbrush, stopping frequently to swat a mosquito or free their fishing rods from a wild grape vine. Then they went down a steep ravine, grasping roots and treading on stony footholds. Even with Joe's help, Dee fell several times, but was still laughing when they reached the stream.

The stream was a scene of wild Adirondack beauty. Giant boulders divided eager currents that slowed to gently swirling pools. Sunlight filtered through the wavering leaves and danced on the rocks like the footsteps of unseen elves.

They used golden, perfectly round salmon eggs for bait. Joe showed her how to flick the almost weightless line onto the water and let it drift to the shadows at the edge of the pool.

Within minutes Dee had her first fish. He fought and struggled and ran with the current. When she finally reeled him in she was surprised he was only about five inches long. But he was a trout, a brook trout, and a native at that. He was not one released by the Fish and Game Department simply to grow and be recaptured. They carefully freed him from the barbless hook and sent him scurrying to the safety of a rocky grotto.

They caught several more of the little fighters, all too small to keep. Then they climbed the rocks upstream in search of the next pool. Here Joe caught a keeper. He was a good twelve inches long, big enough to fry over the fire that night, but in a sudden outburst of compassion, they freed him, too. Somehow it seemed like they should remain here. They knew many fishermen would not agree with them. They didn't care.

By noon they had fished enough.

"Better to quit while it's still fun," Joe observed. "Makes better memories that way."

They returned to camp and swam in the chilly lake, splashing and dunking each other like silly harbor seals.

Towards evening they rowed out to a tiny island. It was no more than a rocky outcropping with one gnarled wind-beaten tree. Had the rock tumbled from a distant mountain or erupted from the earth below? Or perhaps it was a memento of the ice age, left behind by a retreating glacier. Whatever its source, Dee found the island to be a place of fantasy and imagination. She was a pirate awaiting passing ships. She was Robinson Crusoe cast up on its narrow shore. She was a queen in exile from her noble throne.

Then she stared again at Lookout Mountain and her dreams faded into cruel reality. By now there could be no doubt. The mountain was just as blurry as on the day of their arrival.

She wanted to cry. She wanted to beat her fists against the sharp stones. But Joe was there and she didn't know how to begin to explain it all to him, so she held the tears back once again.

All that evening she tried to think where she had gone wrong. Oxygen hurt her eyes. There was less oxygen in the mountains. Her eyes should be getting better. But they weren't. Of course, there were mountains and there were mountains. Maybe she should have gone to the Himalayas. They were higher, they would have less oxygen.... The answer came to her with a jolt. But of course! She hadn't even given the Adirondacks a chance. She simply needed to go higher. She needed to go to the top of Lookout or any other of the peaks surrounding her.

She dug out the trail map the ranger had given them. Lookout Mountain: elevation 4025 feet. Little Squaw Lake: elevation 2200 feet. A difference of over 1800 feet. That had to be the difference. She had to climb Lookout.

She almost asked Joe to take her mountain climbing the next day, then she read the description of the trail on the back of the map.

> The first mile and a half is over rolling terrain and the climb is gentle.... The trail then climbs more steeply.... In the last mile there are pitches so steep you have to use your hands. Only old faint blazes mark the trail here.... Inexperienced hikers should not attempt this climb.

She was sure Joe wouldn't let her go. It was one thing to let her slide down the ravine to the trout stream, although Mums wouldn't have allowed her to do even that. But she knew Joe would refuse to let her climb that mountain. He would remind her in a kind way of her clumsy gait and weak ankles. She would beg and plead, but this time he wouldn't give in.

Still, she had to climb Lookout Mountain. The idea had taken hold of her now. There would be no turning back until the act was accomplished. It became a goal within a goal, secondary even to the promise of healthy eyes. She became Determined and Daring. By nightfall she had a plan.

She curled up in her sleeping bag and listened to the call of the loon. Joe told her that according to Indian legend, it was the cry of a warrior refused entrance to the happy hunting grounds.

In her dreams that night, she was an Indian girl sent by her people to the highest peak to appease the god of the wind. When she came to the top of the mountain a deer came to her from a grove of balsam trees.

"Welcome to our world, Earth Sister. I give you the strength of my legs so that you may run swiftly and gracefully."

A hawk flew down from a barren pine branch and landed on her shoulder. "I give you the sharp vision of my eyes," he said, "so that you may see the beauty of this earth."

Then a giant eagle carried her off the face of the mountain and returned her to the valley below. Her people welcomed her as a heroine and made her a princess in the tribe.

CHAPTER TEN

Climbing Lookout Mountain

She awoke to the harmony of a chickadee and the chatter of the squirrels. The dream had been so real that for a moment the green fabric of the tent became the rawhide of a tepee. Then the sight of Joe's tousled hair protruding from the sleeping bag brought her back to the present.

She sneaked out of the tent and had the bacon sizzling by the time Joe awoke. She presented him with a cup of coffee, steaming and too hot to hold in the tin cup.

"You're a good kid, Dee," he muttered sleepily.

She felt pleased. He would be in a good mood. But then she didn't want to overdo it and let him suspect her of bribing him.

She made her move at breakfast while he was eating his fried eggs, done just the way he liked them; crisp bottoms, soft tops, yolks juicy enough to soak into the buttery toast.

"Joe, would you be upset if I didn't go fishing with you this morning? I think I really would rather stay here and read a book today."

"Of course not, love," he answered, "but there is no reason I need to go either. I'll stay here and read, too." It was the answer she had expected. She did not panic or let the anxiety show on her face.

"Please, Joe, I want you to be able to fish some more. And I really would enjoy staying here alone."

He looked at her strangely, then replied, "Okay, Dee, if that's what you'd like. Does that mean I get out of doing the dishes?"

He was joking but she offered immediately. Soon he was motoring along the western shore and Dee was kneeling on a boulder, leaning over the water, scrubbing the frying pan with gritty lake sand.

Quickly she finished the task, then stuffed her knapsack with candy bars, a peanut butter and mayonnaise sandwich, a pair of binoculars and a canteen of water. Finally, she wrote a note and pinned it to the tent flap.

> *Dear Joe,*
> *I decided to take a walk.*
> *Will be back in time for dinner.*
> *Love, Dee*

She clutched the trail map in her hand and started out. It had all been so easy, she thought. She had been Deceptive, but in her excitement she felt only a little bit bad about her lie. She was also counting on Joe fishing all day and not finding the note until she was well on her way back to the campsite. The first mile was along the highway to a small parking area where the trail began. There the trail was clearly marked with a sign that nearly made her turn back.

TRAIL TO LOOKOUT MOUNTAIN. CAUTION!
STEEP CLIMBS AHEAD. TRAIL SLIPPERY WHEN WET.
DO NOT ATTEMPT CLIMB IF THUNDERSTORMS FORECAST.

But the sky was clear and the trail looked so easy and gentle. She decided she could turn back if it became too difficult or if any storm clouds appeared in the sky. Shortly, she came to a wooden box fastened to a tree. Another sign.

HIKERS. PLEASE REGISTER DESTINATION AND TIME
IN AND OUT.

"I thought I was going into the wilderness," she mumbled. "This is like walking along Central Street." But she dutifully wrote in the logbook: Dee Gardner, Lookout Mountain, August 16, 9 a.m. She guessed at the time. She looked over the list in the book. No one had been on the trail for three days.

The trail stayed gentle for awhile. She went past giant oaks, maples and beeches. Once, she caught a blurry flash of red in a bush to her left. She thought it was a cardinal. Maybe if she saw the bird on her way back, when her vision was better, she could be sure.

She rested at the first stream. It was a noisy, playful brook, the kind you read about in story books. Then she went along a ridge that swung up and down enough to make her work hard, but never enough to make her stop to catch her breath. She paused by a giant hollow beech. One side was open, forming an inviting seat. She leaned back and gazed upward at the musty tunnel, wondering how many raccoons and opossums had made their dens there.

The stream came back to greet her. The cool sparkling water looked safe to drink, but she sipped from the canteen instead. She passed through more of the giant woodland, then abruptly came upon a beaver pond. At first she thought it was some man-made pool, but the tooth-marked stumps and dome-shaped water huts were unmistakable trademarks.

The trail had vanished at the pond's edge, but she followed some faint muddy footsteps to the left and crossed on top of the springy stick-dam. She wished she could see one of the furry creatures gnawing on a sapling or slapping the water with its flat tail, but the pond was quiet except for the ripples of the water bugs.

She crossed the stream a third time. It was only half as wide as before, but now it rushed down a waterfall in a terrified plunge to escape some monster of the mountain. She grabbed a fallen trunk tightly and inched across, stopping on the far side to empty the water from her sneakers.

The trail became steep. Her ankles were sore and tired, but she tried her best to ignore them, concentrating on the ache in her arms instead. It was like the tricks she used to play on her body after her ankle surgery. Her skin would itch under her casts, so she would close her eyes tightly and pretend the itch was really on the tip of her nose. She could scratch it there. Sometimes it worked.

The trail seemed to go on forever. The peak was somewhere above her, but how much above her? Sometimes she thought she was almost there, but the path had only leveled off to climb sharply once again.

The map had said it was six miles to the top. She had to have gone that far. Six miles was from home to the library and back, then back to the library again. That didn't seem so far, but up here distance seemed to have lost all meaning. Maybe she had gotten on the wrong trail. But there had been no side trails and the red markers reached out to her from the tree trunks at her side. She played another game; three trail markers then rest, then four and rest. At six start over.

In spite of her fatigue, she gave no serious thought to turning back. This was more than a battle for her eyes. It was also a battle for her scarred, imperfect ankles. Even more, it was a battle in her determined mind.

Now new rewards urged her onward. Turning around, she could glimpse the lakes in the valley below and the mountains of the next range. She pressed on for a better view.

The giant oak and maples were gone now. Here the trees were dwarfed, almost like a larger version of the Japanese bonsai plants Mums had shown her once. The ground, too, was more barren with more stones emerging from the skimpy topsoil. Rocky ledges protruded across the trail. Once, the

49

trail narrowed to a treacherous foothold with a sheer cliff on her right and a frightening drop-off to her left.

When the pathway widened again, she flopped against a wind-beaten balsam, drank long satisfying gulps from her canteen and ate the Snickers bar the man at the diner had given her. It seemed like years ago. After that she felt better.

She even dozed a little, using her knapsack for a pillow. It was only a short nap, but when she awoke, her ankles had already become stiff. When she stood up, she lost her balance and toppled to the ground. It was something that happened to her often; when she tried to roller skate, when she played tennis, when she had been stupid enough to take ballet lessons. Now she found that her humiliation was not any less just because she was alone.

She massaged her tender, swollen ankles. This time she considered going back, but the thought of failure hurt even more than the pain in her joints. Perhaps she would have turned back had she known what was ahead. But she was determined to reach the top no matter what the cost. She climbed on.

It was no longer even a trail. It was a climb straight up on her hands and knees, pulling herself onward one rock at a time. The red trail markers were no longer friendly. They leered at her. They pushed her back. They whispered, "You can't do it."

She went on.

The sweat was pouring down her face now. The sun had climbed past its midday apex and drifted to the western slopes. Its hot rays scorched her back. The ones that missed her reflected off the rocks and burned into her face.

Once, she glanced back and was petrified of the steep drop behind her. It was less frightening to climb upward than to go back down. She would worry about that later. Maybe the eagle of her dreams would carry her to safety.

She passed through a rocky chasm, barely wide enough to squeeze through. The damp rocks of the walls had a sweet musty smell. Daylight was a jagged tear at the top.

Then suddenly and without warning she was there. There could be no mistake. This was no cruel hoax or illusion leading to another climb. This was the top. All around her was open space.

She stared to the east, the north, the south and the west. As far as she could see there were mountains and valleys dotted with lakes. They were all kind of fuzzy, but she wasn't sure if it was because of her eyes or the natural haze.

She took the binoculars out of her knapsack to look more closely. It brought the horizon closer, but no matter how much she focused the lens, the scene remained blurry. Still, she could recognize the distant landmarks. The rim of darkness caused by the wall of the binoculars was hardly noticed, for it only added slightly to her usual loss of vision in her periphery.

When she looked to the west she could see Little Squaw Lake and then to her astonishment she could even pick out the faint outline of their campsite and the little rocky island.

My eyes have to be better here, she thought. But when she took off her glasses, even the balsam at the plateau's edge became a greenish blob. It looked like a Christmas tree wrapped in a garbage bag.

Time, she thought. A little more time. She concentrated again on the little island. She refused to believe that its outline was revealed to her only because of the powerful binoculars.

She stretched out under a scrubby oak, again using her knapsack as a pillow. It was so different from the oak at home, she thought. She missed Donkey. The sun was kinder now. Its gentle rays danced across her body, urged on by the playful breezes that ran up the mountainside from the valley below.

CHAPTER ELEVEN

Disaster

Dee wasn't sure how long she had slept. Maybe only for a few minutes, more likely for at least an hour. The clang of the garbage bin penetrated her dreams but she barely moved. Then it returned, a crash that split the air and jarred the rocks beneath her. She awoke with a start expecting the bear to be upon her, but Little Squaw Lake campground was miles away.

The cool mist splattered on her face even before she saw the angry dark clouds. Then the splinters of spruce flew past so quickly that her mind scarcely associated the terrifying event with the brilliant flash that had preceded it.

She knew she had to get off the mountaintop quickly, but even before she had taken the first few precarious steps down the rocky incline the storm had arrived in its full fury. The rain washed over her face and fogged her glasses. She paused to wipe them off with a corner of her soaked shirt. Within seconds they were opaque again.

Somehow she made it to the chasm and the relative safety of the chimney-like walls. She leaned against the side, trying to catch her breath. Then a bolt of lightning struck the rim. Rocky splinters cascaded around her. The sound of thunder was so loud she was certain the rocks had crushed together. But she was, for the moment, all right except for the ringing in her ears and a few scratches on her shoulder where the shale had pierced her T-shirt.

She escaped that prison and continued downhill. She knew she was moving too fast, for her feet slid whenever she took a step, but she could not help it. Somehow a fall down the steep incline seemed better than to be devoured by the awful lightning.

The rain mixed with her sweat. Her glasses refused to stay in place. Every few seconds she had to push them back up on her nose. But at least the storm was losing some of its fury. The rain was a little less intense, the thunder a little less frightening. Dee even chanced a thought that she might escape alive.

Then everything went wrong at once. In a cruel dying gesture, the storm let loose a final bolt of lightning that exploded just above her. Dee cringed to avoid the terror. Her foot slipped and she lost her balance. Even then she might have recovered, but at that moment her glasses slipped from her face. The overriding importance of those glasses had become a part of her reflexes. She lunged to retrieve them.

The fall went on forever. Somewhere along the way the harsh jarring bumps against the rocks seemed to become softer, a mossy cushion on every other boulder. The moss was like a soft body that eased, but did not take away, the painful bruising of her flesh. In an absurd moment of hope she thought the eagle had come to rescue her. Then a second later she knew she was dying. The fall down the cliff was intertwined with the angels carrying her off to heaven.

Then there was silence. No thunder, no crushing rocks, no screeching wind invaded her ears. I'm Dead, she thought. I'm the final big D word. There was no panic in the thought, just a mild curiosity. She felt detached from the whole event as if she were standing beside herself watching it happen.

Then she remembered the times she had been unkind to Grandma Oster and the lie she had told Joe that morning. Oh no, she thought, I'm not good enough to get into heaven. She wondered if it was too late to repent of her sins.

She slowly opened her eyes and looked right into the face of God. A hundred jumbled thoughts raced through her brain. He's blurry. I thought my eyes would be all right in heaven. He feels like a person. He looks awfully young to be God. I wonder if there is oxygen in heaven? Why doesn't he talk to me? If I ask him maybe he will perform a miracle and cure my eyes. God wears a T-shirt! God wears a Pepsi T-shirt!

"Joe? Is that you?"

"Are you all right, honey?"

"I-I think so. I-I can't see very well. Maybe I have a concussion."

She wasn't sure what a concussion was but she had heard of people having one after a fall.

"You've lost your glasses, Dee. Maybe that's why you can't see."

"Oh. I guess you're right."

Slowly she disentangled herself from Joe's arms and tried one leg then the other. Incredibly, they worked. She felt her left arm with her right hand. It, too, was intact. She knew her right arm must also be all right if she had just used it. To be certain, she felt her right arm with her left hand, starting at the shoulder then finally squeezing each finger in turn. She sat up. She stood up. She was a little puzzled that her body worked so well after having been dead just a few minutes before.

"Help me find my glasses, Joe."

"They are right here, honey."

She reached for them but he held them back.

Even with her distorted vision she could see the twisted, bent frames and the shattered glass. She remembered the party she had planned to follow her eye transplant. Now everything had gone wrong. But even that didn't matter so much. She had been rescued. Joe was here. She would be safe now.

The storm had faded to the east and the thunder was a distant roll. She didn't really fear it now, but the memories it brought made her uneasy.

"Let's get out of here, Joe."

"We can't, Dee."

She looked at him, surprised. It was weird. He had rescued her. Did he plan to abandon her here? Then she saw the look of pain on his face.

"It's my ankle, Dee. I think it's broken."

CHAPTER TWELVE

Stranded on the Mountain

Dee helped Joe slide up his pant leg, then slowly unlaced his hiking boot and eased it off. The ankle had swollen into a purple spongy water balloon. In spite of Joe's reassurance that it only hurt a little, she knew the pain he must be feeling.

It's probably worse than having surgery, she thought.

Suddenly she realized what a horrible thing she had done. Here they were, stranded on a mountaintop, she without her glasses, Joe with a broken ankle.

"Oh, Joe," she sobbed. "I'm so sorry. This is all my fault."

"Shh, honey," he comforted her, "everything is going to be all right." But he, too, knew they were in trouble.

Although Dee felt like she had fallen down a cliff, she had only fallen down the steepest part of the trail. In a way it was fortunate, for here at least they found a reasonably level patch of ground, free from the jagged stones. With help from Dee, Joe managed to scoot over to the trunk of a maple. Dee huddled next to him, still clutching her useless glasses.

"How did you know where to find me, Joe?"

"Oh, Dee, I should have known you were up to something this morning. I suspected it when you didn't want to go fishing, but then I thought you really did want to read your book today. After I fished for a couple of hours, I got to worrying about you. So I came back to check on you.

"It didn't take me long to figure out where you had gone. You've been staring at this mountain ever since we got here. But, thank goodness, you signed that trail registry.

"I should have taken time to get one of the rangers and have him come with me, but I thought I could probably catch up to you. I hurried as fast as I could but you must have climbed this mountain much faster than I ever expected you would. When that thunderstorm struck, I was really worried. Then I saw you coming down those rocks. I called out to you, but you couldn't hear me over the noise of the storm."

"So you were right below me when I fell," Dee concluded.

"Yeah," Joe answered ruefully, "I was so close."

"You broke my fall but I smashed your ankle," Dee said.

They were both silent for a moment thinking about how close Joe had come to rescuing her, but how much worse it might have been if he had not been there at all.

"What are we going to do, Joe?"

"Well, we are going to make the best of it, Dee, but somehow I'm afraid you are going to have to go for help unless some other hikers show up. It's too late to go tonight. It will be dark long before you can get off the mountain. Now get me the first aid kit out of my knapsack."

He took adhesive tape and patched Dee's glasses together as best he could. The frames were still crooked. The right lens was gone completely, but the left, although cracked, was still in place.

"There. That's the best I can do. Try them on."

It wasn't much. Her right eye was her best. Now it was useless. Her left eye gazed at a world divided into spider web segments, but at least she could see.

"Now find me a branch to splint my leg," Joe commanded.

She did as she was told and soon had the leg taped to the trunk of a poplar sapling.

"Okay," he grinned, "you got any food in that sack?"

She pulled out the remaining candy bars and sandwich and they shared them like children on a picnic. Joe even seemed to enjoy his half of the peanut butter and mayonnaise sandwich. Maybe his broken ankle has changed his taste buds, Dee thought, remembering the day in the park with Miss Vaughan. But she didn't really believe that. In fact, the idea seemed childish now.

They spent the night huddled together for comfort, not for warmth, for in spite of the high altitude and the thunderstorm, the air remained mild and humid. Their soggy clothes dried slowly. Dee had gathered enough dead branches for a fire which they managed to light in spite of the dampness. They kept it going more for the coziness it provided than for the scant hope that the wisp of smoke would be seen from the valley below before darkness fell.

They took turns telling little stories about the woods and the mysterious folk who lived there. They only talked about the friendly ones. They were not up to any scary stories.

Then Dee told Joe about her eyes; the transplant disappointment, the library search with Miss Vaughan. Joe listened quietly. In fact, Dee realized he had never even asked why she had climbed Lookout Mountain. Instead he just held her hand and let her spill out the whole story. Finally, she told him about her idea that the mountain air would cure her eyes. She finished with another sobbing apology.

"Oh, Joe, this is all my fault. I've gotten us into an awful mess."

He did not scold her. "We're going to be all right, Dee. And it is not all your fault. Your mother and I should have been more understanding and we should have explained things better to you. Parents aren't always the wisest people in the world. You see, your mother and I often feel guilty

59

about what happened to your eyes. The doctors told us that your being born prematurely wasn't because of anything we did or failed to do, but I guess we still blame ourselves sometimes. So we just don't talk about it very much.

"I know we should have explained it all to you long ago, but we just kept putting it off. And I guess sometimes we forget how fast you are growing up. We forget you are old enough to understand these things now. You shouldn't have had to look up the answers by yourself, although I'm proud of you for having done that. Still, we should have helped you."

He hesitated a moment, uncertain as to whether or not he should say more, then continued. "There is something else you need to know, Dee. Living in the mountains where there is less oxygen isn't going to help your eyes. The doctors explained it to your mother and me. The oxygen could only hurt your eyes at a time when they were still being formed. Once your eyes grew or matured, the amount of oxygen you breathe makes no difference at all. I'm sorry, Dee, but climbing Lookout Mountain or taking airplane rides isn't going to help."

Dee was almost surprised that she felt so little disappointment. Perhaps deep inside her she knew all along it was a futile hope. Perhaps her disappointment was overshadowed by her concern about getting off the mountain and getting help for Joe. Maybe just feeling close to Joe was the most important of all.

Dee even slept off and on during the night. The balsam boughs she had gathered eased the discomfort of the uneven soil and her mind was simply too exhausted to dwell on their predicament or the trudge down the mountain the next morning. Whenever she awoke, she heard Joe's grunts of pain. She doubted if he slept at all.

In the morning, Joe actually had to shake her to wake her up. Only a faint rim of sunlight seeped from the distant hills. The rest of the sky was covered with thick gray clouds.

"You better get started soon," Joe said.

She nodded. "I wish I could make you coffee first."

He smiled. "I'll be okay. But thanks for thinking about it."

She arranged his makeshift bed of Balsam boughs one more time and checked his ankle. It looked even worse than the night before. As she stood up, she stumbled over an unseen tree root and nearly collapsed on top of him.

"Dee! Can you see well enough?" Joe asked, alarmed.

"Sure, Joe. I just stumbled over that root." She started toward the trail. Joe called to her, "Dee."

"Yeah, Joe?"

"I love you, kid."

She went back to his side and hugged him tightly, no longer trying to conceal the tears in her eyes. "I love you, too, Joe."

Then she was on her way. She moved carefully among the rocks, but tried to act casual until she was out of Joe's sight around the bend in the trail.

CHAPTER THIRTEEN

The Long Journey Down

This time she did not feel bad about the lie she had told Joe. It would not do to have him worry about her eyesight all day. But the truth was she could barely see at all. Her right eye was almost useless without her glasses. Her only vision in her left eye was a small area in the very center and even that was crisscrossed with the cracks in the lens. It was like walking down a long dark tunnel with light only at the far end. She constantly had to look from side to side to be certain she wasn't stepping off the trail.

At least she had already descended the worst of the trail. There was only one spot she was afraid of. That was the narrow part with the cliff on the one side and the drop-off on the other. She came upon it quickly, dreading it, but glad it would soon be past. It was worse than she had remembered. She looked for a way to bypass it. There was none. She sat on the trail trying to gather her courage. Then she thought of Joe beside the maple tree. She remembered how much more swollen his ankle was that morning than last night. She knew she had to get help as quickly as possible.

She faced the edge of the cliff, closed her eyes tightly and inched along one small sidestep at a time. When she reached the other side, her knees were shaking and her heart was pounding, but she only dared to rest for a moment.

She found that the best way was to concentrate on finding the red trail markers with her left eye, for the trail was now wide enough that there was little danger of sliding down a ravine. The worst that could happen would be that she would bump into a tree. However, she could not see the protruding stones and roots at her feet and she had little judgment of the steepness of the trail. Consequently, she frequently lost her balance and tumbled to the earth. Her body already ached from the bruising of the day before. These new jolts seemed to penetrate all the way to her bones.

She felt like she had reached a major milestone when she came to the first branch of the stream, although she knew she still had miles to go. She had been thirsty all night, but had saved her water for Joe, pouring the remainder from her canteen into his when he wasn't watching. Now she filled her canteen and drank long, satisfying swallows. The water tasted sweet and pure with no hint of the chemical aftertaste of city water.

The sky was even more cloudy now. Big dark rain clouds threatened to erupt at any moment. She felt their presence more than she saw them. She worried about Joe on top of the mountain, but her sensitive ears detected no distant roll of thunder.

At least most of the trail was downhill. That, in part, made up for her impaired vision. Then, too, there were the familiar milestones of her progress of the day before; the stream, the hollow tree, the blackberry patch. At the blackberry patch she took a moment to pick some of the juicy, seedy berries. But her vision was so bad that she kept getting her fingers caught on the thorns and she also remembered how much bears liked to feed here, so she hurried on her way.

Her glasses broke as she crossed the beaver dam. Or rather, the last precious fragments of her left lens crumbled and fell through the interwoven sticks that formed the lattice-work of the dam. There was no particular reason for it to happen here. Dee had not jarred or poked them. The remaining pieces had simply fallen out of the frames.

She crawled on her hands and knees to the far edge of the pond, then sat down and cried iong sobbing wails of defeat and self pity. Then she became angry; angry at herself, angry at the doctors who had given her oxygen, angry at all the kids in school who had ever laughed at her and called her Google Eyes.

Her anger gave her determination. She hurled the useless frames into the beaver pond, then set off again along the trail. But she couldn't see the trail, or the trail markers either. What she could see was a blurry, wandering brown ribbon of dirt winding through a smear of green. Slowly and deliberately, she followed it.

She had to get help for Joe. That thought prodded her at every step. If she failed, he might die. It was a lot of responsibility for any twelve year old child. To add the handicap of near-blindness was cruel.

Her sense of isolation increased. The ache in her bruised, imperfect ankles was almost overwhelming. Her sensitive ears became a hindrance rather than a help. Every sound was magnified by her imagination into something horrible and dangerous. The drone of a mosquito became the approach of a swarm of deadly wasps. The rustle of leaves in the wind became the stalk of a hungry panther. The splash of the brook became the roar of thunder.

She went on.

Then came the most frightening sound of all. It grew louder and louder. It sounded familiar but in her confusion she could not identify it. She wanted to turn and run, but instead she lost the path and wandered to the edge of what looked like a swamp of pitchy black quicksand.

It was the end, Dee thought, a fate that reminded her of the fall down the steep rocky trail. This time Joe would not be there to rescue her. This time she would die for sure. She would sink into the quagmire and drown, or the approaching monster would devour her in a single gulp. She wondered which would happen first.

But then she realized the quicksand was actually hard and warm and the roar of the monster ended with a shrill dying screech, like a dragon slain by a knight in shining armor.

"Are you all right?"

The lady jumped from her car and ran to Dee's side as a pair of four year old eyes stared in wonder at the girl crouched by the side of the road.

Dee could only sob, but eventually blurted out some meaningful words. "F-father. B-broken ankle. M-mountain."

"There, there, it will be all right, honey. Get in the car and I'll take you to the ranger station."

It was a ride of less than a mile. Her tears were already drying and her voice reasonably calm by the time they got there.

The ranger radioed for the emergency helicopter, then took her to the campsite for her extra pair of glasses while they awaited its arrival.

CHAPTER FOURTEEN

Rescued

When Dee put on her glasses, she felt like she was stepping into a new fantasy world. They were like the 3-D glasses she had worn over her regular glasses at a movie at an amusement park once. Indeed, later she said that the rest of that day seemed to flash by like the images on a theater screen. Even when it was over she wasn't quite sure what was real and what was imaginary.

The glasses, of course, were the same as the ones she had broken, but in the short time she had been without them she had almost gotten used to a nightmare world where all objects blended together into one indistinct mess that resembled the finger paintings of a three year old. Only when she had her glasses again did she realize how bad her eyesight was without them.

The helicopter landed in a meadow near the ranger station. Usually it was against the rules to take passengers along, but the pilot thought Dee might be helpful in locating Joe. She crouched under the revolving blades and ran to the door, tightly holding the hand of the paramedic. A few moments later she was staring down at the top of Lookout Mountain. It seemed impossible they had gotten there so quickly, yet there was Joe, waving his arm from under the maple tree. Then the paramedic went down the rope ladder and splinted his leg. Soon Joe hobbled up the ladder and crawled in beside Dee.

A minute later the mountain was behind them. It all happened so fast that it made her long journey up and down that precipitous mountain seem ridiculous.

They landed on a big red cross in the parking lot of a small hospital. Dee stayed close to Joe in the emergency room, in the X-ray department and even when the doctor applied the cast. He would have to spend the night, but the nurses set up a cot in his room so Dee could stay with him.

To her surprise and embarrassment, she found out she was a hero. Everyone praised her for her bravery. Newspaper and TV reporters appeared to interview her. They had learned of the broken glasses from the forest ranger, but were uncertain of how much that had hindered her. In response to their questions, she only remarked, "It wasn't all that bad. I could still see some."

It was a private matter, she thought, although she suspected she would have been even more of a hero had they known she was nearly blind without them.

When she returned to Joe's room the phone rang. It was Mums. Mums! Dee had forgotten all about her. Joe had called her when Dee had been talking to the reporters and now she was calling back to let them know that Mr. Wolinski was bringing her there. They would leave in a few hours, but it would be early the next morning before they would arrive.

"Dee," Mums said, "I'm proud of you."

Dee was certain she wouldn't have said it if she knew it had been all her fault that Joe had broken his ankle. But it was too hard to explain that to the voice in the telephone receiver. It would all come out soon enough, she thought. So she only mumbled, "Thanks, Mums."

Dee could hardly believe how nice everyone was to her at the hospital. She had been treated well when she had her surgery on her ankles, but that experience was associated with pain, intravenous needles and the bitter taste of anesthesia. Perhaps, also, people were more friendly in this small Adirondack hospital.

One of the nurses took her to the cafeteria for a hamburger and a glass of milk and later brought her a big dish of chocolate marshmallow ice cream.

She was no longer worried about Joe. They had been reassured by the doctor that the ankle would heal, and with the help of some pain pills, he rested comfortably. Both of them were tired from their ordeal and by nine o'clock they had fallen asleep. Occasionally during the night Dee awoke to the sound of footsteps as the nurse checked Joe, and once she heard the siren of an approaching ambulance. Each time she drifted back to sleep. The rough damp bed on Lookout Mountain seemed far, far away.

Mums arrived early the next morning. There were tearful hellos, then Mr. Wolinski took them to the campsite to get their car and help them pack their things. He took the boat and most of the camping equipment in his car so they would have plenty of room for Joe in the back seat.

Dee walked down to the lake for one last look around. That's where Mums found her, staring at Lookout Mountain, tears streaming down her cheeks.

Mums put her arms around her. "That's the mountain, isn't it, Dee?"

Dee nodded but said nothing.

"Come on, Dee," Mums said kindly. "I know what will cheer you up."

They drove back into town and pulled up at the only restaurant. It was a stately inn with a spacious lawn and rocking chairs on the front porch. Inside, the dignified elderly guests were eating their poached eggs and cream of wheat. Mums ordered strawberry milk shakes and French fries for both of them.

"Nothing like some junk food when you're feeling low," Mums whispered to Dee. "Besides, this place needs a little perking up."

They giggled softly at the stares of the other diners when their food was served. Suddenly, Dee felt closer to her mother than she had in her entire life. She had a feeling Mums knew all about her reason for climbing the mountain even though she knew Joe hadn't had a chance to tell her.

Joe was ready to be discharged when they got back to the hospital. He stretched out on the back seat of the Toyota with his cast propped up on a pillow. Soon they were on their way home, along the winding, tree-lined highways, toward the little towns with strange names.

When they passed the sign that said LEAVING ADIRONDACK STATE PARK, Mums announced, "Well, the next time you two decide to go camping, I guess I'll just have to come along to keep you out of trouble."

Dee smiled. The image of Mums sleeping in a tent or cleaning a fish didn't seem so strange anymore.

CHAPTER FIFTEEN

Up to Something

Six weeks later Joe's cast came off. By that time Dee was back in school. Most of the kids had heard about her adventure on the mountain. No one, not even Billy Snodgrass, called her Google Eyes anymore. There had been a party for Miss Vaughan when she returned from England. Dee told her all about the Adirondacks. Miss Vaughan said that sounded a lot more exciting than her trip.

Grandma Oster had come for a one week visit. They got along better this time and once Grandma had even called her Dee instead of Dorothy. Dee thought she must have done it by mistake, but she wasn't sure.

The broken glasses had been replaced. Her new frames were different. The lenses were the same.

Life was pretty much back to normal, except Dee sensed her parents were up to something. They would not tell her what it was.

One October morning they announced they had a surprise for her. They would all be taking a short trip the next day. She would miss a day of school; it had been cleared with her teacher. She pestered them all evening but learned nothing.

The next morning they got in the car and drove, of all places, to the hospital. Dee couldn't figure out why they were coming here. Maybe I'm going to have a brain transplant because I'm so Dense, she thought. That idea was absurd. Then she had the horrible thought that she needed surgery on her ankles again. But she knew it wouldn't be like her parents not to tell her about it ahead of time.

Mums explained as they walked up to the front door. "We know you've been here before, but we thought you might like to see where you were born."

A lady in a starched pink uniform with a red name tag that said VOLUNTEER on it met them at the door. She had a real name, too, but Dee missed it when they were introduced.

She took them up the elevator to the maternity ward. A dozen red-faced bodies wailed in unison as they approached the nursery window.

"Almost feeding time," Miss Volunteer said.

For a moment, Dee imagined she was there to adopt a baby brother or sister. One cute little dark-haired baby caught her eye. She decided she would make a nice little sister. She peered at the blue sign on the side of the bassinet: BABY BOY JOHNSON. 6 lb., 3 oz., 18 1/2 inches. She decided if she couldn't tell a boy from a girl she wasn't ready to adopt one yet.

There was a small room to the side of the nursery. It was empty except for a small table on wheels with a metal canopy hanging over it.

"That is called an infant warmer," Miss Volunteer explained. "Sometimes babies are put in there if they are sick or if they are getting too cold in their cribs."

"You were in this room for a couple of hours right after you were born," Mums told her. "Then a doctor and a nurse came and took you away in an ambulance to another hospital where they take care of premature babies."

They saw the room where Mums had stayed. It looked like the room Dee was in after she had her ankle surgery. On the way out, Dee was allowed a quick peek in the delivery room where she was born. The green tiles and bright lights looked cold and forbidding.

Dee shuddered and said, "Yuch. I wouldn't ever want to have a baby in there." Then she immediately regretted the statement, thinking she had probably insulted her host.

But Miss Volunteer only smiled and said, "Many mothers feel that way also, Dee. We have a new room called a birthing room that you might like better."

Indeed, the birthing room was almost a pleasant place. The bed looked more like the one she slept in at home. The wall was papered with giant daisies and soft music drifted through a speaker. Dee decided it might not be so horrible to have a baby after all.

They thanked Miss Volunteer, then left the hospital and drove out of town, where they got on the interstate highway and headed west.

"We are going to the hospital where you were taken after you were born," Joe explained. "You see, you were so tiny and so sick that the doctor thought it would be better if you went to a hospital where they had special doctors and nurses who take care of premature babies."

"It was very hard to see them take you away, Dee," Mums told her. "But I knew that was what was best for you."

"Then I had to leave your mother to be with you," Joe continued. "That was hard, too. I wanted to be at both places at the same time."

"After I got out of the hospital we came to see you almost every day," Mums said. "For a long time we couldn't even hold you. All we could do was put our hands in the incubator and touch you. Several times the doctors called us in the middle of the night and said you had gotten worse, so we would get up and drive two hours to be with you. Each time you would start getting better again. I suppose our being there didn't really have anything to do with it, but we liked to think that we were helping you."

Dee had never heard her parents talk like this before. It made her feel sorry for them. She felt bad she had caused them so much trouble, yet she knew that wasn't why they were telling her these things. As Joe explained to her, "We just want to help you to learn about yourself and your eyes."

It made her feel much closer to her parents.

She watched the farmland beside the interstate highway and the little towns that scurried by. She felt as if she were sitting in a time machine, watching the world go by. She thought of herself as becoming younger and younger. First grade now, then glimpses of herself as a stumbling toddler. Soon she would be lost in the innocence of her infancy, watching events that were supposed to have been driven from her memory forever.

It was all a bit scary, and at the same time fascinating, like watching an old horror movie, knowing it could not harm you, but not quite believing it enough not to be frightened anyway.

The interstate increased from two lanes west to three lanes. The interchanges became closer and closer together with the big signs announcing the next exit at one-half mile instead of two miles. Trucks sandwiched the Toyota into the center lane. Graffiti peppered the underpasses. Then they got off the interstate highway and headed along a city street.

CHAPTER SIXTEEN

The Children's Hospital

At first it didn't look like a hospital. It was too big with too many towers interconnected by walkways. To Dee it looked more like the nerve center for some large corporation or perhaps the government offices of a small country.

Then she saw the imposing red letters: EMERGENCY ROOM. Five ambulances were lined up outside, each with its rear wheels perfectly aligned against the wide curb. Some displayed their impatient waiting with the nervous flash of their emergency lights.

Joe parked the Toyota on the roof of a parking garage. Dee hated parking garages. Her eyesight dimmed with the sudden darkness and the narrow, twisting ramps seemed to squeeze her mind. She could never remember having told Joe about her dislike, but he seemed to know about it. As always, he passed one parking space after another until they emerged in the sunshine again.

They went down the elevator to the street and walked along tree-lined sidewalks, past park benches filled with medical students eating bologna sandwiches dug out of crumpled brown bags. They went up the steps leading to a large gray stone building. MILTON BARNES CHILDREN'S HOSPITAL was inscribed above the door. Dee wondered who Milton Barnes was. She thought there must be a lot of sickness in this city to need a separate hospital just for children.

She glanced up and counted the rows of windows. There were five. Just this one building was bigger than the whole hospital at home. It made the little hospital in the Adirondacks seem remote and insignificant. But the lobby

74

lacked the friendly comfort of the hospital where she had spent the night with Joe. Here, groups of people, some bored, some frightened, huddled behind magazines used only to protect them from the stares of others. Two ladies at a desk crisply issued directions and visitor's passes.

Her parents seemed to be caught up in the hurried pace of the interns and nurses. They rushed her down the corridor and into a crowded elevator. It was a local, stopping at each floor to discharge and receive passengers. It reminded Dee of the bus she and Joe had taken in New York City one time.

They got off when the light announced "four." Again they went down a long carpeted corridor. This time they went to a row of offices. They stopped at one that said, DEPARTMENT OF NEONATOLOGY. Dee's tongue stumbled over the last word when she tried to pronounce it. She asked Mums in a whisper what it meant.

"Ne-o-na-tol-o-gy," Mums whispered back. "It's a word for doctors who take care of sick newborn babies."

Dee understood. She still couldn't pronounce it, though. She wondered why doctors had to use such big titles.

Inside, everything seemed relaxed and friendly. Pictures of babies lined the walls. Three doors opened beyond the small waiting area. In the corner of one room Dee saw a large stuffed pig.

Dee thought this place was like a quiet oasis, isolated from the rest of the hospital. There was a home-like atmosphere here that she had not seen anywhere else in the busy complex.

Mums spoke briefly to the receptionist who smiled and said, "Oh yes, we were expecting you."

She took them to the room with the stuffed pig in it and asked them to wait there. Dee didn't even have time to look around the small office before a tall middle-aged man with a

75

jet-black handlebar mustache entered the room. He was wearing blue pajamas.

"Mr. and Mrs. Gardner. How good to see you again," a voice boomed out at them. "And, of course, you must be Dee."

"This is Dr. Lazari," Joe explained. "He took care of you when you were a baby."

A flood of emotions entered Dee's mind and bounced from one side of her skull to another, ending in a muddled tangle of conflicting thoughts. Dr. Lazari! Of course! She felt stupid for thinking he was wearing pajamas. He was in a scrub suit, the kind the surgeons wore when she had her operation. Then deeper thoughts surfaced. This was the man who had taken care of her when she was a premature baby. This was the man responsible for her lousy, stupid, nearly-blind eyes.

She tried to feel angry at him, but somehow she could not. She wanted to cry. She wanted to run out the door and down the stone steps and past the ambulances with the flashing lights and go home and hide in her room. Instead she mumbled something that sounded like, "Hurro, tractor linzi."

She felt stupider than ever. No wonder Billy Snodgrass used to call her Google Eyes. She was Dumb, Dodo-brained Dee.

Joe and Mums were saying something about leaving her alone with this man, but the words were only garbled syllables in her brain. Suddenly, she realized they were gone.

CHAPTER SEVENTEEN

Dr. Lazari

"Well, Dee, it sure is good to see you again."

"D-don't you have to take care of your patients?" Once again she had spoken without thinking. She really hadn't meant to be rude.

But the grin that sneaked up around the corners of his mustache never left his face. "Nope. Not today. Have to have an afternoon off every now and then. Dr. Andersen is taking care of my patients today. Say, how do you like my pig?"

Suddenly the panic was gone. He really is a person, Dee thought. He even talks like I do. But, of course he does, Dee, she told herself. What do you expect him to do, speak in Latin, you Dummy?

Aloud she said, "Gee, he's really neat. Where did you get him?"

"The nurses gave him to me for my birthday last week," he said proudly.

"They say they did it because I always come around at night and beg their food from them," he whispered confidentially. "But between you and me, I think they should be glad there is someone who appreciates their lousy baking."

Dee giggled, then glanced around the room. One whole wall was covered with pictures of babies and children.

"Are these your patients?" she asked.

"Not now, but all of them were when they were babies." Again she could sense the pride in his voice.

"Let's see." He glanced along the top row, removed one and showed it to her. "You recognize this person?"

A skinny little kid in droopy shorts clutching a teddy bear stared at her. She recognized the teddy bear before she recognized the child.

"Why that's me!" she exclaimed.

"Sure is," he replied. "Your mom and dad sent that one to me when you were two years old.

Soon they were chatting about school and vacations and mountain climbing. She listened in awe to Dr. Lazari's stories about rock climbing in the Tetons. Soon Dee found herself telling him about her climb up Lookout Mountain. She was nearly to the end of the story when she realized she was on dangerous ground. She was afraid he would ask why she had gone up the mountain by herself. That would bring up the whole subject of her eyes, a topic she definitely wished to avoid. She finished the story hurriedly with a disjointed account of the night in the hospital with Joe.

Dr. Lazari didn't seem to notice her discomfort. "Wow!" he said. "That really was some adventure. I'd like to climb that mountain some day."

Then his voice became more serious. "Dee, your parents told me you have a lot of questions about your eyes. I think I can help you understand better what happened to you. I'm not sure how you feel about this. Maybe you don't feel comfortable talking about it with me. Maybe you feel angry at me because I'm the one who gave you the oxygen. If you do, Dee, that's all right. I understand. I'm not going to try to force you to talk about all this, but I would be happy to try to answer any questions you might have."

The panic started to rise in her again. The lump in her throat stuck there like a wad of Double-Bubble gum that refused to go up or down. But she felt no urge to run away, and most important of all she didn't feel Dumb. When this kind man told her he understood, she believed him.

He continued talking, not giving her a chance to answer. She was grateful for that.

"I'd like for you to come with me, Dee. I want to show you some things that I think will interest you. Later, if you still want to, we can talk about your eyes."

They walked down the corridor and through a set of doors that opened automatically as they approached. Suddenly all the hectic activity of the hospital was upon them again. Nurses and doctors quickly walked past them as if hurrying to catch up to the voices that called them from the loud speakers over their heads.

They stopped at a big spotless sink where Dr. Lazari showed her how to wash her hands using a soapy brown brush. Her hands felt soft and wrinkled when she was finished, like they did when she dawdled too long with washing dishes. There was a faint smell of iodine that made her feel clean and good.

Then Dr. Lazari helped her into a white gown. It was much too big for her. She felt like she was the Pillsbury Doughboy without a hat. Dr. Lazari rolled up the sleeves as best he could, then from somewhere produced two safety pins and hemmed up the bottom. He stood back to admire his work.

"There," he said, "I guess that will have to do. We are going into the Neonatal Intensive Care Unit, Dee. It is where we take care of the smallest and sickest premature babies. It is where you were for several weeks after you were born."

Then he lowered his voice and whispered as if they were involved in a great conspiracy. "Children aren't supposed to go in there, Dee. If anyone asks who you are, tell them you are one of the new medical students."

He winked and Dee giggled.

They went through another set of sliding double doors. Inside was an amazing scene. It was more bewildering than anything Dee had ever watched on TV or at the movies. It was even more confusing than the nightmares that sometimes tormented her in her sleep.

CHAPTER EIGHTEEN

An Amazing Place

The center of the room was filled with plastic boxes placed on top of blue-green cabinets. The wall was lined with different equipment. Dee vaguely recognized them as being similar to the infant warmers she had seen at the hospital in her room. Each box and warmer was surrounded by more equipment that either had lights flashing on and off or gave out soft beeping sounds. Some did both. She thought at first they had entered some strange mechanical control center for the hospital, then she became aware that at each station, in each box or warmer, there was a baby.

So this is where I was as a baby, she thought. She expected to feel some sort of sense of having been there before, like they talked about in the movies. She remembered they even had a word for it, some sort of French phrase, although she couldn't think what it was. But she had no recall of this place, no feeling of any familiarity whatsoever. If Dr. Lazari said she had been here she would just have to take his word for it.

She realized he was talking to her. "It's kind of scary, isn't it."

She nodded.

"We get used to it, of course," he continued, "but I always feel sorry for parents when they have to come in here for the first time. Of course, the babies can't say anything and they don't remember what happens to them, but still, I often wonder if it isn't frightening to them, also."

Several of the nurses smiled at Dee. Then one of them who looked a little older than the others walked over and said, "Hello, Dee. It sure is nice of you to come back and visit us."

"You-you took care of me, too?" Dee whispered.

"I sure did," she told her. "You were in this corner right over here." She pointed to one of the plastic boxes that Dee learned were called incubators.

They walked over to the incubator and Dr. Lazari said to the nurse working there, "Mr. Grayson, this is Dee Gardner, our newest medical student." Everyone laughed and Dee felt more at ease.

She peeked into the incubator. There was a little body inside, although at first Dee wasn't sure if it was a person or some sort of strange hairless animal. It was smaller than Donkey and had a shrunken little face with reddish wrinkled skin. It looked a little bit like a large dried apricot. Thank goodness I didn't blurt that out to Dr. Lazari, she thought a second later, for just then the scrawny little arms and legs began to wave like little windmills and she realized this was a real baby, a real live premature baby.

"Her name is Melissa," Dr. Lazari told her. "She is about the same size you were when you were born."

"R-really?" Dee exclaimed. "I-I was that small?"

Suddenly she thought the little baby was rather cute, but she still had trouble believing she had ever been that tiny.

"How much does she weigh?" Dee asked.

Dr. Lazari picked up her chart and replied, "Let's see. Today she weighs almost two pounds."

Two Pounds! Dee thought it could hardly be possible. She weighed sixty pounds. She was thirty times bigger than the little baby even though she was smaller than all of the

82

other children in her class. That also meant she had grown thirty times the size she was when she was born. She knew most babies weighed about eight pounds at birth, or at least that was what Jimmy Barton weighed when he was born last New Year's Day. The Bartons lived next door.

She looked in the incubator again at this exciting little person. Little tubes and wires seemed to be coming from everywhere, making it hard to see her very well, but what caught Dee's eye was the tiny diaper taped to her bottom.

"Hey, where do you get such tiny diapers?" she asked. She was thinking how neat they would be for her dolls.

"Oh, a lot of special things are made for premature babies; premature diapers, premature clothes, even special small nipples for their bottles," Melissa's nurse told her.

"What are all those other things on her?" Dee asked.

Dr. Lazari explained them patiently. "The tube coming out of her mouth goes into her trachea or windpipe. It is connected to this respirator that helps her lungs to breathe."

He pointed to a red and blue machine beside Melissa's incubator that seemed to have a thousand dials and lights and little needles that jumped up and down.

"Was I connected to a resp-repator, too?" Dee asked.

"Res-pi-ra-tor," he corrected her kindly. "You sure were. For almost a month."

He next pointed to a needle stuck into Melissa's hand. "This goes into one of her veins. The fluid in this bottle has sugar water in it. That is the only nutrition we can give her now, but soon we can give her some of her mother's milk, a few drops at a time, through a tube that will go down her mouth into her stomach.

"These little round things on her chest are called electrodes. They detect her heartbeat and send messages to this machine here so that if it beats too slow or too fast we will know about it at once."

"Hey those lecrodes have smiley faces on them," Dee exclaimed.

Dr. Lazari laughed. "It's just something to make her parents feel a little better when they come in to see her. All they can do is touch her and hold her hand for now. She is too sick for them to hold her. It was the same way when you were born."

Dee remembered what her parents had told her that morning. She again felt sorry for them, having to sit beside her, wondering if she would get better or not. Now she understood a little bit better why Mums didn't like to talk about it.

"There is one other thing I want to show you, Dee," Dr. Lazari continued. "Melissa is breathing oxygen through her respirator. She has to have oxygen because her lungs are very sick. But if we give her too much oxygen we might hurt her eyes."

He pointed to another little wire taped to Melissa's toe. It, too, was connected to another machine.

"This is called an oximeter," he explained. "It tells us how much oxygen is in her blood and helps us know how much to give her."

They walked through the Neonatal Intensive Care Unit and looked at the other babies. Dee couldn't believe there were so many premature babies. Some looked just like Melissa, but others were much bigger. Dr. Lazari explained that sometimes babies were sick when they were born, even if they weren't prematures.

In another room the babies were in cribs and dressed in regular baby clothes. Some of them were being fed or rocked by their parents. Dr. Lazari told her these babies were almost ready to go home.

Dee felt like she could stay in the nursery for days without becoming tired of it, but it was time to go back to Dr. Lazari's office. She walked over to Melissa's incubator for one last look at this reminder of the first few days and weeks of her own life.

"Good luck, Melissa," she whispered. "I hope your parents love you as much as Joe and Mums love me."

CHAPTER NINETEEN

Ice Cream and Answers

As soon as they sat down in Dr. Lazari's office, a secretary walked in and handed each of them a strawberry swirl ice cream cone.

"You like strawberry swirl, too?" Dee asked.

"Hate the stuff, but somehow everybody thinks it is my favorite flavor."

Dee knew he was only kidding by the way he ate the cone.

"Well, Dee, are you ready to talk about oxygen and eyes?"

"I-I think so," she replied.

"Dee, sometimes it's very hard to explain medical things to people, even to grownups. That is because medicine can be very complicated. But I think that sometimes doctors just use that as an excuse. Maybe they feel uncomfortable talking to their patients, especially if things don't go right.

"I'm going to try to explain to you what happened to your eyes as best I can. I know you won't understand it all, but it will give you something to think about. You can even come back at some other time and we can talk again, if you want. Or maybe you will have to wait until you are older before you can understand all of it.

"Many years ago doctors learned that oxygen was very important for premature babies. It helped them with their breathing. It helped keep their brain cells healthy and many times it saved their lives. However, the doctors didn't know as much as they should have about the oxygen and the way it worked. They didn't know how much to give and they didn't always know which babies should receive it. But since oxygen is a natural element in our environment and everything they did know about it indicated it was good, they thought it couldn't possibly do any harm. So they gave lots and lots of oxygen to all premature babies.

"Well, they were wrong. When the babies got a little older, many of them had trouble seeing and a lot of them were blind. When the doctors looked into the eyes of those children, they saw changes that they called retrolental fibroplasia. Those are two awfully big words that really mean scar tissue behind the lens of the eye. They didn't know what was causing this new eye disease for quite a few years. Finally, someone discovered it was due to the oxygen. Does this make sense so far, Dee?"

"I think so," Dee replied She thought of Melissa getting oxygen through her respirator. "Why do you still give babies oxygen then, if it hurts their eyes?"

"That's a good question, Dee. When the doctors learned that oxygen could hurt the eyes, they did stop using it, or at least they didn't use so much of it. The problem was, many of those babies needed lots of oxygen. Sure, there weren't as many babies with eye problems then, but there were more babies who either died or grew up to be mentally retarded from a lack of oxygen."

"I guess the oxygen is both good and bad at the same time," Dee remarked, remembering the words of MIss Vaughan.

"That's exactly right. When the doctors realized that, they tried very hard to give just the right amount of oxygen; enough to keep the brain and other body organs healthy, but not so much that it hurt the eyes. After that they saw a lot fewer babies with eye problems and more of them were healthy in other ways, also."

"So I was born before the doctors knew that," Dee said. "I got too much oxygen and that is why my eyes are damaged." It was not an accusation, just a bitter realization that she had been born at the wrong time.

"No, Dee," Dr. Lazari said gently, "we understood all that when you were born. We tried to watch the oxygen levels in your blood very carefully. You were even attached to a machine similar to the one you saw in the nursery today that always told us how much oxygen to give you. As far as we know you always had just the right amount of oxygen."

"Then why were my eyes damaged?" Dee insisted.

"Dee, this is going to be very hard to tell you, because I don't know the answer for sure. We know that if the amount of oxygen in the blood is too great it can cause eye damage. And yet there are still some babies who get eye damage even when the blood oxygen is kept at a normal level or even if they don't breathe any extra oxygen. We think there is some reason in addition to prematurity and oxygen that causes some babies to get retrolental fibroplasia. Unfortunately, we don't know what the reason is. Scientists are still doing research to find out. Maybe they will discover the answer soon. I know this must sound confusing and complicated to you, Dee. I'm sorry, but I really don't know how else to explain it."

It was confusing, Dee thought. Sometimes during the conversation she felt like they were talking about some patient in a movie script, someone she didn't even know. Then it came to her with a jolt that they were discussing her and her eyes. Yet, she thought she understood most of what Dr. Lazari had said.

"Is the oxygen still hurting my eyes?" she asked.

He smiled. "What you really want to know is if it would help if you lived someplace where there is less oxygen."

"My father told you about that, didn't he?" Dee felt a little bit angry at Joe, but mostly she felt Dumb again.

"Sure," said Dr. Lazari, "but that wasn't such a dumb idea. Some scientists thought of that years ago. The only problem is it doesn't work. You see, the only time the oxygen could hurt your eyes was when you were still a premature baby. When you became older, the amount of oxygen you breathed didn't affect them one way or the other. The reason you have trouble seeing now is because of the scar tissue left behind when the damage was done."

Although she was disappointed, she felt somewhat better now. At least he didn't think she was Dumb. And that gave her the courage to ask the final, most important question. She took a deep breath.

"Dr. Lazari, is there anything that can be done for my eyes or will I have to be like this for the rest of my life?"

"Dee, I'm really not sure what to tell you. Right now there is nothing that can be done except for the glasses you wear. But there are a lot of new operations that have been tried lately. None of them are good enough yet to help your eyes, however. I don't want to promise you something that won't come true, but it wouldn't surprise me if sometime, maybe in five or ten years, somebody would develop an operation or other treatment that will help you to see better."

They sat in silence for a few minutes, then Dr. Lazari asked, "Can you think of anything else you would like to ask me, Dee?"

She smiled at him. "Sure. Would you like to visit me sometime? I would treat you to a strawberry swirl with sprinkles."

"You bet I will, Dee. Maybe someday we can even climb a mountain together."

CHAPTER TWENTY

The Birthday Trip

Dee Gardner. Lookout Mountain. June 2. MY BIRTHDAY! She wrote that in big capital letters. She looked at the watch Mums and Joe had given her that morning and made the final entry: 8:16 a.m.

The trail really hadn't changed much. The leaves were younger and greener than in August, and hundreds of little spring wild flowers poked out from among last autumn's layer of fallen leaves.

The stream had changed the most. It was at least twice as wide as before, and the stepping stones were covered by a rushing torrent. There was only one way to cross. She took off her shoes and socks, rolled up her pant legs and waded the icy waters. When she reached the other side her toes were numb, but the sun dried and warmed them quickly.

This time she approached the beaver pond cautiously and was rewarded with a glimpse of brown fur and the unmistakable thud of warning. The water lapped over the top of the dam in places, but she could still cross. She held her glasses tightly against her face, remembering her last journey here. The spare pair were in her knapsack, just in case.

A vine she could not identify had started to entwine the hollow beech. Perhaps it had grown from a stray seed dropped by a passing hiker. She gazed upward at the hollow trunk, wondering again if this had been the winter den of a raccoon.

She inched along the narrow cliff. It still made her uneasy, but at least this time she could see her progress. Then there was the place where she and Joe had spent the night.

She found a few sticks of balsam. The needles had disappeared long ago.

At last there was the final climb to the top, one rock at a time. It was no easier than before, but somehow there was a greater reward in the challenge, more pleasure from the effort.

She paused after passing through the chimney chasm, giving Mums a hand over the final few steps. Joe followed a moment later. The sweat poured down their faces, they gasped for breath, and their muscles ached, but all three of them were smiling.

"Whew!" Mums whistled. "That was even worse than I expected. But you know, Dee, I'm glad I did it."

"Look at that view!" Joe exclaimed. "This is terrific. It's even better than from a helicopter."

They took out the binoculars and Dee showed them the important landmarks: Little Squaw Lake, Kunjamuk Mountain, Panther Peak, Crooked Pond. The gentle breezes swirled around them. This time there were no forbidding clouds on the horizon.

Then Joe and Mums made Dee close her eyes and count to one hundred. When she opened them there was a one-layer chocolate fudge birthday cake, slightly squashed from its journey up the mountain in a knapsack, but complete with thirteen flaming candles.

"Happy birthday, Dee," Joe and Mums told her.

She blew out the candles and they had a party right there; peanut butter and mayonnaise sandwiches, Granny Smith apples, lemonade from Joe's canteen, and, of course, the cake. Mums said the strawberry swirl ice cream would have to wait until later.

They gave her another birthday present. Dee protested that the watch was enough, but she opened the package eagerly. It was the Nepal-Pasteur volume from a set of encyclopedias. Joe explained that the rest of the set was in the car at their campsite because Mums had refused to lug all of it up the mountainside.

"We still want you to go to the library, Dee, but we thought it would be easier if you had your own encyclopedia at home," Mums told her.

Dee kissed them both and told them it was the best birthday she had ever had.

"Dee," Mums told her softly, "we would have given you new eyes if that would have been possible."

"I know, Mums, but it is really okay. I'm learning to live with what I have. Maybe I'm growing up a little bit."

At last it was time to start the long trek back down the mountainside. Dee told Joe and Mums to start out. She would be along in a few minutes. She gazed again through the binoculars at Little Squaw Lake with its rocky islands. Then she took off her glasses and looked at the majestic distant peaks. They were blurry and indistinct. It was as she had expected.

Yes, she told herself, I'm learning to accept my eyes as they are, but I'm not giving up. Sometime, somehow there will be a way to make them better.